GODS AND MUMMIES, OH MY!

CRYMSYN HART

Purple Sword Publications
Tucson, AZ

GODS AND MUMMIES, OH MY!
Copyright © 2014 CRYMSYN HART
ISBN 978-1-61292-118-1
ISBN 10: 1612921183
Cover Art Designed by Anastasia Rabiyah
Photographs Copyright Wisky
Edited by Brieanna Robertson and Jessica Glanville

Published by Purple Sword Publications, LLC
Tucson, Arizona, USA
www.PurpleSword.com

Prologue

Kalliope scanned the shop for the tenth time, worrying her pen. After six months, everything was finally the way she wanted it. Chase, her friend and ex-boyfriend from high school, owned the small shopping plaza. At first, he wanted to give her the entire building. She attributed that to the effect her magick had on people and the universe. Ever since she'd become a true witch, things in her life had become easier and fallen into place. She had talked him into taking whatever inventory she had in the shop for payment. Gods forbid she got too greedy and the universe decided to throw another obstacle in her way. Well, it really wasn't the universe, but the gods who controlled said universe. After the assassination attempt on All Hail last year, her life had settled down. There hadn't been any more crazy, serpent-haired goddesses attempting to take over the world or insane sun gods trying to kill her.

A lot had occurred over the past two years. There was a real cheesecake god, and his name was David. No matter how immune she was to godly charms, nothing could beat his power over women. Every once in awhile, she had found cheesecakes on her counter she did not buy, and they were not a product of her magickally self-stocking fridge and cabinets. No matter how much David tried to woo her with his luscious delights, her heart was stuck on one particular hot sun god who was always naked. She was still getting used to the idea of being naked with him. However, Kalliope had no problem staring at his perfectly formed bottom and his ever-ready equipment. Just thinking about him made her hot. She blushed picturing him. He was tan, sculpted perfectly, with evergreen eyes, and a smile to die for. He always knew when she was in trouble. When they were together, he read her thoughts before she even knew what she wanted, bringing their lovemaking to another level.

"If you think about me any harder, the whole place might combust." Arms entwined around Kalliope's waist, squeezing her slightly. A supple voice tickled her ear. She closed her eyes and enjoyed the attention. Silky lips kissed along the line of her neck. Lugh's firm length pressed against her backside. Goosebumps ran over her body from the chills he gave her.

It'd be so nice to have a break.

"Why not take one then? You *are* the proprietor of the store."

Kalliope turned in his grasp, surprised to find he wore clothes. The red T-shirt emphasized every muscle, and his black jeans accentuated all the right curves, including the bulge of the erection he sported. Her cheeks burned when she thought about the things he had done to her in the past. All it took was one simple touch. Without saying a word, his hand slipped under her shirt. Once the tips of his fingers caressed her flesh, Kalliope gripped her thighs together to stay focused and keep her mind on this planet. Golden light flared behind her eyes and fused her chakras together while his power surged through her, touching her most intimate places only he was allowed to explore. Her pen clattered to the floor. She ground against him to feel his firm shaft. He slowly planted kisses along her neck, teasing her with quick flicks of his tongue. His fingers trailed upward to cup her breasts. A moan passed over her lips. His mouth left warm imprints behind when he moved to another part of her throat.

"Do you know how much I want you right now, Kalliope?" he whispered in her mind.

"How much?"

One hand left her breast and eased under the waistband of her blue jeans. She was already so wet it would've been easy to let her jeans fall to the floor or magick them away and have him deep inside of her. His fingers touched her hidden bud, and reality vanished. Surges of heat rushed along her nerves. Her fingers dug into the meat of his calves to hold herself steady from the orgasm clutching her.

"Wow. Oh boy—I…ah…can see I have to come back later." A familiar voice sounded in the store.

Kalliope bit her lip. Her cheeks seared from being interrupted in such an intimate act. She opened her eyes and saw Lugh's lopsided grin. It seemed he was used to getting caught.

"Later." He chuckled. *"Besides, we'll have more time to go over things then."*

"What things?"

He gave her a quick kiss on the cheek and didn't reply. She felt the echo of his presence from the absence of his warmth when he stepped away. She smoothed her hair, straightened her clothes, and then turned around. Kalliope had completely forgotten she had told Anna to come over and help her go through tons of bridal magazines. *What does a witch wear to a wedding where the majority of the guests are gods and mythological creatures?* Flidais offered to have the Fates weave a dress for her, but she declined. *I really don't want any more obligations with the gods. Everyone wants their two cents.* It wasn't every day a witch married a god.

"No, Anna. Come on in. We...were…ahh—"

"Just playing a little game of strip poker." Lugh beamed.

Anna's gaze dropped to the tile floor. Kalliope tried to zip up her jeans when she noticed the zipper was broken. Closing her eyes, she pictured herself in a broom skirt and when she opened her eyes, she was. She smiled. Her new powers were great, and she was glad she was getting the hang of them. Lugh ran his fingers along her sides until she squirmed.

"I'll leave you two ladies alone. Let me know when you're done. There's someone I want you to meet."

"Not another god. Haven't we seen all the gods on the Council yet?" In order for them to marry, they needed the approval of all the major god pantheons. So far, they had seen the Japanese gods, the Celtic ones, the Greek ones, and a slew of others all because she wasn't completely human anymore.

He kissed her nose. "I know, but we have to be sure. You know that All Hail is paranoid that you'll become a full-fledged goddess and it'll go to your head. Maybe you'll want to take his place or even knock me off."

She ran her hand over his crotch and sent a bolt of power through him. He closed his eyes and sighed. Kalliope loved to watch him shiver. "That would never happen. I don't wanna be Mistress of the Universe. And how could I live without you? Fine, rules are rules. I'll let you know when we're done."

Lugh clutched her bottom. "Good. Because if you don't, I'll send some of those penis-shaped oranges you love so much."

Before she could reply, he was gone. Kalliope sighed. *I hate it when he does that.* She shook her head and focused back on her coven sister. Anna heaved a stack of catalogues onto the counter. A shiver of fear went through Kalliope. *More pages to flip through. Oh joy. How many paper cuts am I going to get today?* She flashed back to the heaps of magazines she had already gone through. "Let's get this over with."

Her coven sister giggled. "You know, it could be worse."

She laughed at that. Even though she'd informed her coven about her trials of saving the world, they really didn't know the half of it. "Oh yeah. It really could be."

Chapter One

Kalliope rolled over and reached out to find the spot that Lugh had occupied was empty. She groaned and buried her head in the pillow because she was all toasty and cozy. Her body protested coming out of its warm cocoon, but her head told her she had to get up. A list a mile long of wedding preparations waited for her. *Another fifteen minutes. Then I'll get up and face the world.* Her eyelids grew heavy once more. In a daze, she heard the clanking of dishes near her. The enticing aroma of bacon and coffee drew her into wakefulness, and she opened her eyes.

Standing in the doorway was Lugh dressed in nothing more than a red apron and carrying a tray. He set the tray down and sat on the edge of the bed. He ran his hands over her back. Kalliope groaned, hoping he would continue and massage her back. Then he yanked the covers down. Cold air blasted across her skin. She squealed. Lugh laughed. She wanted to slap him one, but her scowl melted once she witnessed his lopsided smile and warm green eyes. Lugh was tanned perfection, and it still amazed her that he had chosen her. Lately, her betrothed had tried to act more human. His chest glinted from the bacon grease, and a smudge of flour streaked across his nose.

"Are you awake yet?" He brushed his fingers over one of her nipples. They hardened instantly against her shirt. He went lower and slid his hand over her stomach. She tried to ignore the smooth sensation of his palm on her flesh. Kalliope trembled and stuck her tongue out at him.

"If you're not careful, I'll find ways for you to use that." He leaned in and kissed her lightly so she could taste the maple sweetness on his lips. She wrapped her arms around his neck and pressed her mouth against his, hoping to taste more than maple syrup. He continued to kiss her for a few more moments until he pulled away and licked her nose.

Kalliope jerked and wiped her nose. "Eww. All right. I give. I give. Breakfast smells wonderful." She sat up, and Lugh set the tray in her lap. He lifted the fork and began to feed her. Once she bit down, she tasted apples. At that moment, she knew the pancakes had been made by her Aunt Constance. The woman might have been a ghost, but she visited her on occasion and made her things out of apples. On the second bite, she stopped him.

"Something wrong?"

She shook her head and drank a sip of the coffee. "Nothing, but I know you're planning something. Constance made the pancakes, so what do you have up your sleeve?"

He grinned and held out his arms. "See, no sleeves, so nothing to be up them."

She ran her fingers over his arms, barely squelching the lust she had for him. "You know what I mean." She crunched on a piece of bacon and set some aside for Humphrey.

"You know me all too well, my love. There's someone who wishes to meet you."

She rolled her eyes. If she had to meet any more long-distance relatives, dethroned gods, or another pixie, she was going to scream. Planning a wedding to a god was difficult. So far, everyone had a say, and she meant everyone. Zeus had offered up Mount Olympus for the ceremony. Flidais and Nas were arguing over flower arrangements and why orange orchids would be better than white ones. Morgaine had volunteered to design the dresses for all the bridesmaids, who included her coven, Morgaine,

Flidais, and Nas. The cake was taken care of by David the cheesecake god along with Constance preparing all the food. Music was provided by the Muses. They still needed to pin down the exact menu and the theme of the wedding. Nas had suggested unicorns for gifts to all the wedding guests. Flidais argued that was over the top. Kalliope didn't care as long as it got done.

Dread filled her when she contemplated a dress. Everyone had an idea of what she should wear, but she hadn't found anything quite right. Now Lugh was requesting she meet someone else. *I thought getting married would be easy. Why don't we just elope?*

"Who is it and why?"

The expression he wore was grim. "I've been trying to hold her off for as long as I could, but if we don't get her approval then I don't know if we can get married."

She stopped mid-bite. *Not get married. I'm so not hearing this right now!* She had saved the world from bean curd eating goddesses last year, and now she couldn't marry the man she loved? "You're a god. I thought no one told you what to do. And didn't you tell me that everyone approved of us getting married? Shit, I died and saved All Hail from a godly coup. Doesn't that count for anything?"

He walked his fingers up her leg. She watched a line of his energy go up her skin. "I know you did, and everyone does, but she was on vacation hanging out with the Mayans. She's the last goddess on the Council that you haven't met."

Kalliope lifted the tray from her stomach and got out of bed. She began pulling the brush through her locks, trying to keep her temper under control. She didn't need anything exploding in flame or a torrent of oranges falling around her. As she stared at her reflection, the mirror rippled. An arm holding a sword appeared out of the glass. The silver sword glowed with a blue light with runes etched into the blade. Kalliope sighed and took the weapon. Immediately, her boiling emotions simmered. When she glanced down, she was in warrior princess garb.

"Thanks, Excalibur."

The sword knew her moods and helped to calm her. No matter how many times she left it in Avalon, it always returned to her because she was its chosen champion. She laid the sword on her dresser and willed her clothes to be jeans and a T-shirt since she had candle making to do today. She ended up in a white linen dress with a scarab necklace and no bra. It didn't help that the neckline plunged to the middle of her stomach. She tried to will the costume away or at least change it, but nothing worked.

"I'm meeting an Egyptian goddess, aren't I?"

"How did you guess?"

"I've kinda gotten a hunch for these things over the past couple of years. Who is it? Mut, Sekhmet, Baast?" She glanced at the red diamond on her finger. It was quite literally a piece of his heart. A flare of warmth shot through her. Her anger melted completely away when she looked deep into his eyes. She couldn't remain mad at Lugh. Kalliope loved him too much and didn't want anything to go wrong between them. *What's one more goddess going to hurt? I've seen dozens of them so far.* "Fine, but I promised Theresa I'd watch the twins. This date is important to her."

"Good. I'll let her know to come."

"Whoever it is, please tell her to be on time. Who is it anyway?"

Lugh's eyes lit up. "You'll know her when you see her. Tell her I said hello."

"Did you sleep with her, too?"

"We had our moments. We're still close, but she can be overbearing, so please be careful."

"You do realize how odd it is for me to meet all the women that you've slept with, right?"

"Does it make you uncomfortable?"

"I didn't say that, but most human women would be jealous as hell."

"Nas was, remember?"

Kalliope recalled all too well the thorn prison Nas had put her in. "Yeah. How could I forget?"

Lugh smiled and kissed her while his thumbs fondled her tight nipples. She gasped, but before she could get any satisfaction, he was gone. "Figures."

At that moment, she heard crunching near the bed. She glanced over and saw Humphrey munching on the bacon. He stopped when he realized she saw him. His mouth spread into a wide grin so that she could see his pearly whites. Then his gaze traveled from her face to her chest. His eyes bulged, and his jaw dropped. In an instant, he disappeared, and reappeared snuggling against her breasts.

"So luscious and so ripe. I just want to squeeze—" His webbed feet traveled down her breast.

Kalliope threw him across the room once he began feeling her up. "Ick! Humph, what have I told you about crossing the line?"

The turkey-sized bullfrog hovered in the air, suspended by white, fluffy wings. "I know. I've been a baddd froggy. Please punish me. They're so round."

"I don't want to hear it. If you're hungry, help yourself to breakfast. Please pop the dishes into the sink when you're done. Come by the shop because I have work for you to do." The frog didn't protest, but batted his eyelashes at her. The complete devotion her familiar had for her was unsettling at times. Out of the corner of her eye, she saw Excalibur glow, so she picked it up. "Fine, you can come too, but no warrior princess. It's bad enough I'm in this outfit. Can you be smaller?"

In its own way, the sword was sad. She still hadn't figured out its otherworldly artificial intelligence, but she could sense its moods. It shrank into a tiny sword about six inches long with dull edges. Kalliope wound her hair up into a bun and slid the sword through it to hold it in place. Snagging another piece of bacon, she envisioned the candle shop and walked through the bedroom door. Once she emerged, she was at work. Nas lingered behind the counter with a wide smile on her face and a blank stare that she gave all the customers.

"Welcome to Wicks. How...oh it's just you," Nas said. Her smile melted away, and she slumped down in her chair. Kalliope knew the goddess was bored, but she was the one who had volunteered to watch the store. Nas had wanted to get into the groove of being human, as she put it.

"Gee, thanks for the awesome welcome. It makes me want to buy something." Kalliope scanned the shop. Ever since she'd added the bath line and become a witch, her inventory was difficult to keep on the shelves. She made it, and *poof*, she got an order. Between the shop and the Internet site, her supplies were selling out. If only she had more time to make things. With the craziness of the wedding revving up, she was lucky if she got to breathe. Lugh suggested she will her candles into existence, but Kalliope enjoyed doing things the human way. Besides, the wax made her hands soft and took her mind off everything else going on around her until someone broke her reverie.

"So, what's with the Egyptian garb? You going on a tour of the pyramids?"

Kalliope rubbed her hands over her arms. "No. Lugh says one of the Egyptian goddesses wants to meet me. I suspect I'll be getting a visit tonight."

Nas's expression fell. "Oh shit. I forgot about them. They're one of the older pantheons besides the Greeks. You have to be careful. They can get really plucky, and I wouldn't trust them."

"Great, just what I need to hear. What happens if I don't get their approval?"

Nas lowered her voice. "It would be bad. They can't take away your powers, but they can put you in hell if you don't pass their tests. I don't know. There's never been a marriage quite like yours."

Kalliope trailed her fingers over a large piece of quartz. The energy in it flared to life and tingled up her arm. She didn't dwell on the fact she wasn't wholly mortal anymore. Ever since she'd let Lugh heal her when she was on the brink of death, she'd been different. He'd pushed so much of his power into her that her very makeup had changed. She found herself pressed in from all sides when she was out in the world. It was more than a claustrophobic feeing, but a wrongness. Morgaine was right when she said she would be more comfortable in the other realm or Avalon, where the magickal energies were more in tune with her own now.

The shop, her home, and the houses of her coven members were the places she didn't feel out of place. Lugh wanted her to move out of her apartment and into a house near the woods, but he didn't understand mortgages and moving. It wasn't like she had to deal with traffic because she could think of a place to go, and when she walked through the door, she would be there. However, if she was thrown into some Egyptian purgatory with no magick, she wondered how she would escape.

"Hopefully, I'll knock 'em dead, and they won't find me lacking. What can they do? Weigh my soul?"

The door opened and a woman pushing a baby carriage came in. Theresa was all dolled up and ready to go out on a date. The first one she'd had since her break up with her husband. Kalliope took whatever excuse she could to watch the twins. Besides, her coven sister was still dealing with her powers and those of her magickal children. Once she saw Kalliope, she opened her mouth.

Kalliope put up her hand to stop Theresa from asking her what she was wearing. "Save it. Long story."

The question died on her lips. "Okay. Ahh...you sure you can handle these two little culprits?" The babies cooed when Theresa kissed him. They waved their fingers, and a couple of crystals lifted up and floated toward them. Kalliope plucked them out of the air before the girls could turn them into ladybugs, which they had done before. Immediately, large tears formed in their eyes, and their faces screwed up. Before they could begin crying, Humphrey popped into the shop. He hovered in mid-air and made faces at them. The twins were the second loves of his life.

"I think we'll be fine. Who's the lucky guy? You never told me."

Her friend bit her lip. "He's not exactly your run-of-the-mill guy."

Kalliope steered the twins and the stroller toward the back office of the store. In there, they had a playroom all set up. "Hmm. So, what kind of guy is he? A biker from a traveling circus? A prince working as an accountant? A hairy man that's really a gorilla?"

Theresa blushed. "No. Shut up."

"So, who is it?"

"It's...we met at the Wiccaning and we've been chatting ever since. He's really nice and—"

"One of the gods! Theresa. I don't have to tell you about getting involved with gods. You know how much hassle I've been going through. Not that I mind, but it can be exhausting."

"Actually, he's not a full god. He's only a demigod at best and—" Nas said from the small hallway that led to the back office.

"Thank you, Nas. That's not the point." Kalliope saw the rage in Theresa's eyes.

"Argh!" Theresa crossed her arms over her chest. The air shimmered around her, and several of the candles next to her were engulfed in flame. Theresa jumped back. Kalliope imagined water on them, and a waterfall appeared to put them out.

"Sorry."

Kalliope waved the smoke away from her face. "Hey, no problem. I understand. I'm not saying don't see the guy. I just want you to be careful. I don't want your heart to be broken. Gods can be fickle."

"You'll be glad to know I haven't jumped into bed with him. He adores the twins and he's a real gentleman. I think it's cool. It's nice to have someone notice me after Stan."

She wasn't going to win this battle. Her friend was stubborn. "I know. Fine. I give up. Go and have fun, but warn him if he does anything to hurt you, I'll have his head on a platter, and I mean that."

Theresa giggled. "Will do, captain." She kissed her cheek and then kissed the babies one more time before she left.

Humphrey stretched out his lips with his fingers until the twins cooed. She watched the twins and wondered what it would be like to have children with Lugh. *They'd be a handful, that's for sure. They'll probably get my magick and his god genes. How would that work?* She shook her head when she noticed her familiar pinging around the room. He flapped his wings in vain to slow down, but his speed only increased. The twins giggled. They wiggled their pudgy fingers when Humphrey began doing figure eights. She laughed, but then the frog clamped his webbed hands over his mouth and turned greener than he already was. After snapping her fingers, the frog appeared by her side on the counter.

"Thank you." He leaned against her and batted his eyelashes.

"No sweat, Humph. Just be careful. These little devils are mischief-makers. Aren't you?" She tickled them, and they burst into peals of laughter.

"I don't think I'm making candles tonight. You'll be too much of a handful. Then again, I could take you to Avalon and let the other priestesses wait on you hand and foot."

"We can make them. I told Flidais that you needed more bath salts. Just leave the supplies."

She eyed the goddess and wondered where the jealous shrew had gone. Once she had saved Nas's life, the goddess had put aside her resentment and they had started an uneasy friendship. Over the months, that camaraderie had deepened and they were getting on pretty well. "Thanks. I'll make sure there's apple pie or cheesecake."

"Thanks. Do you—?"

The door opened and a customer walked in. Standing before them was a statuesque woman with ebony skin. She wore large gold sunglasses, and her hair was done up in an elaborate braid. Her gold earrings brushed her shoulders. Her long nails were painted dark purple with gold tips to match her dress. Kalliope figured she was a model and she was in the wrong town.

"Can I help you?" Nas asked.

The customer scrutinized the goddess up and down. "Yes, I'm searching for a specific candle. I hear this is the only place I can find it." She had a slight accent that Kalliope couldn't place, but she was definitely foreign.

"What kind of candle are you looking for?"

"It's for healing made from lotus blossoms and myrrh." She picked up a crystal, examined it, made a face, and then set it down.

"I'm sorry, but we don't have that candle. We can—" Nas floundered.

The woman took off her glasses and glared at the goddess. "Unacceptable. Impossible. I was told it was here. I must have it now." Her nostrils flared and her dark eyes met Kalliope's.

Nas's magick stirred the air. Kalliope put a hand on her arm to calm her. "Ma'am, I'm sorry, we don't have the candle you desire. If you can tell me what else is in it, I can make it for you. It'd be a couple of days and I can send it to you."

"I demand to speak to the owner."

Humphrey pressed against her back and clung to her dress. She glanced down and saw him peeking out from behind her at the abrasive customer. "I'm the owner. This is the best option I can give you. If you don't like it, please leave." She gritted her teeth and kept her magick in check. The twins screamed at the outburst. Outside, another woman peered into the shop. She was dressed in black with a black veil covering her head and face. Her dark, intense eyes took in the situation inside. *Probably this one's friend enjoying the show.*

"Shut those little cretins up. I need the candle now. Later is unacceptable." The woman leaned over the counter until she was only a few inches from Kalliope's nose. She narrowed her eyes and waited to be challenged.

Kalliope smiled. Nas took the twins out back. She tilted closer to the woman, but stayed within a hair's breadth of touching her. "Please leave before you make me do something that you'll regret."

"You have no idea who you're tangling with." The woman grunted, grabbed her glasses, turned on her heel, and went out the door. Kalliope let out the breath she didn't know she was holding.

"Well, that was fun," she muttered. Humphrey flapped out from behind her. She patted him on the head and wondered what else was going to happen today.

Chapter Two

The day passed and nothing else occurred. Kalliope was glad because the twins were a handful with their magick going out of control. The incident with the irate customer walked out of her mind now that it was closing time. Nas kept the twins occupied, along with Kalliope's magick frog. She took inventory and then ordered what she needed for the coming month and some things that interested her. There were several crystals she had seen that attracted her. Her intuition poked her that she would need them soon. *What that means, I have no idea. I normally don't use them, but things are happening so fast and the wedding is only three weeks away on Lughnashin.*

The holiday named after Lugh. That was the only thing he insisted on regarding the wedding. She couldn't say no. The time had snuck up on her fast. It seemed like yesterday Lugh had been taking her around to the Council to meet everyone. Of course, she hadn't met everybody because they always got distracted at the last minute. That was how the guest list ended up taking so long. They'd go over it, and then he would touch her, and *poof*—off into an orgasmic fugue she would go. She had to be sure they invited everyone to the nuptials because if the wrong god, demi-god, or supernatural being was left off, she would have hell to pay. The last thing she needed was someone with a grudge.

Lugh's warning about the Egyptian goddess coming had her worried. She expected a sandstorm to blow in, or have a sarcophagus delivered to the front door, or a mummy pop up out of the floor. No matter who or when they showed up, she would play nice. No one was going to keep her from the man she loved.

"Hey, you all set for the night?" Nas asked.

"Yeah. I'm good. Tell Flidais I said hi. If you need anything for the bath salts or candles, let me know. David will have a cheesecake for you whenever you want it."

"Thanks."

Kalliope checked on the twins, who were asleep on the floor in the protective circle she had cast in the play area. Nothing could get to them. Her familiar was lying on his back, webbed feet up in the air, and his tongue lolling out of the side of his mouth. She shook her head, locked the door, and turned the lights off. When she did, something fluttered in the shadows. She extended her senses and felt along the darkness for another presence, but found nothing. She started toward the back when the sound came again.

"Hello!"

Golden eyes appeared in the corner and gazed at her. The shadows stretched into a long, black snout with sharp, curved teeth. Her wardings flared to life from the intrusion. The crystals she had placed around the perimeter of the circle she'd cast in the store glowed. The being stepped forward and became a figure about seven feet tall. Whole candles were consumed in flame. Once the light reflected off the ebony fur, she recognized the god. He got to the edge of her circle and stopped. He reached out to her, but when his claws touched the barrier, a blue arc of energy hit his hand. The smell of singed fur wafted through the place. She backed up a few steps toward the play area.

"Hello, Anubis." They had only met briefly when she'd first encountered David. The death god had been playing poker with a couple of gods and didn't like the fact that she was interrupting their playtime.

He didn't respond, but took another step so he was even with the wall, and then collapsed. It was then she saw a gold dagger protruding out of his back. Kalliope dropped the circle and rushed to help the wounded god. She lifted him into her lap and placed her hand near the wound. Her palm came back stained crimson.

"What happened to you?"

Loud shrieks blared all around her from the shadows. She willed the circle back up around them. The candles had burned themselves out, but the crystals had started to shine again. Each second, they got brighter. Formless shapes rose from the darkness and surrounded them.

"Don't let them take me."

"Who are they?" she asked.

The shapes pressed on the perimeter of the circle. Their presence was a heavy weight on her shoulders. If it were a few of them, it wouldn't have been so bad, but there were several dozen all screeching, and she couldn't understand them. Her familiar was stirring. She prodded him again with her magick. Anubis groaned when she examined the wound. She knew of nothing besides Excalibur that could truly injure a god.

"What are they?"

"The entourage of the only thing that can take the essence of a god. We were ambushed. Pull the dagger out. Quickly."

"It'll hurt you."

"Just do it. Before she comes."

Kalliope's heart thumped. The screams were deafening. *What does a death god fear? He's death, for Pete's sake.* She didn't waste any time and grabbed the hilt of the dagger, but when she did, the metal burned her. She jerked her hand back. He would have to deal with the blade for a little longer. Whatever was on the outside of the circle wailed again, getting nearer. She didn't want to get to know it up close and personal. She helped the god up. "Can you walk?"

Anubis nodded. The blood streamed faster from the wound and matted his fur. This close to him, she smelled the deep musk of his pelt. She led him into the back room. The shadows tested the strength of the circle. They surrounded it on all sides. When she delved into the power of the wraiths, she sensed they were the emissaries of something bigger and darker.

"Humph, wake up from those froggy dreams. I need you now!" She sent a jolt of energy along their connection to rouse the amphibian. The bullfrog jolted back to consciousness. His eyes grew large, staring at the death god. She sensed his fear even though he didn't show it. "Protect the twins."

He saluted her. "Sure thing, toots!"

Kalliope ignored his slip of calling her toots. She didn't know how many times she had asked him not to call her any derogatory names. They got to the door. She pictured her living room, and when they crossed the threshold, they were at her apartment. The wards went up immediately. The crystals in the room were pulsating. Her circle was stronger at the house than at the shop. The energy throbbing from the quartz was intense, increasing the temperature in the room by ten degrees. The silence was something she welcomed. She led the god to her couch. She glanced around and didn't see any of the shadows out of place. Whatever was after them hadn't followed her yet.

"Morgaine!" she yelled. Her call echoed through the realms. Kalliope hoped to reach the sorceress on Avalon, but there was no answer.

"No one will hear you. They'll find me and come here, too. You must take me somewhere for sanctuary. All my houses are closed to me."

An image of a large oak tree came to her. First, she had to get the dagger from his back. She clutched the hilt again and immediately pulled her hand away. This time, overwhelming pain shot up her arm. She glanced at her palm and saw a scorch mark on her flesh. Her fingers began to tingle and go numb. The red diamond of her engagement ring glowed. The numbness left her and the radiance subsided. However, she was still left with a pins and needles feeling in her fingers. Gritting her teeth, she conjured a towel, wrapped it around the dagger, and then pulled it out. When she dropped it on the floor, it turned her carpet black where it landed.

"What was with that thing?"

"It was a cursed blade. Meant to hurt gods, but not kill. Humans, it can kill. Please, they are almost here. I must get to a safe place."

"No one's going to get through my circle. Come on. I know where to go." She strengthened the circle, willing all of her power into it. In her mind, she envisioned a pristine glade with an enormous tree and a clear blue pool in the center of it. Kalliope slung the god's arm over her shoulder. On the other side of her living room, the clearing came into focus. She placed her hand on the barrier of the circle and was about to drop it when she heard a howl in the corner. She glanced back. Shadows pressed against the circle, but within the twisted mass of darkness, another pair of eyes stared at her. They were huge and almond-shaped. A large, three-taloned hand stretched out from the wall and into her circle. She felt it penetrate the barrier almost as if it were nothing. *What the hell? Nothing's ever come through my circle. I was able to hold back Cromm before. What is going on?*

"She's here. We have to hurry," Anubis growled.

Kalliope dropped the wall and crossed into the dell. Before she did, she felt the talons rake her leg. She and the god fell onto the grass. With all her might, she closed the circle again in her world. The image of her living room disappeared, and they were alone in the hollow. It was night here. The moon was only a slim crescent suspended in the sky, but the will-o-wisps gave off enough illumination that she could see. The gashes in her calf were bleeding pretty badly, but she ignored them for now and hobbled over to the pool. Peering down, the only things that she saw were the long strings of the plants waving in the current beneath. She passed her hand over the still water. The surface clouded over and then the shop came into view. Humphrey was dressed in a soldier's uniform and carried a bayonet. He was patrolling the edge of the circle, but she didn't sense any danger at the store. She didn't want to chance it, though. Moving her hand over the tarn again, the scene changed to that of her coven sister. She was being nibbled on by her demi-god date.

"Danger, Theresa," she whispered.

The wind kicked up and carried her warning. The woman broke her kiss and looked into the night. Kalliope knew she'd gotten the message. She pulled her consciousness back to the meadow and saw Anubis was resting on the outcropping of rocks by the pond. Kalliope shivered at the cold breeze that came up. She glanced around and saw the outline of a woman in the tree line. There was just enough light to show she was dressed in all black with a veil covering her face except her intense eyes. Kalliope thought she seemed familiar, but when she blinked, the woman was gone. Yowls reached a crescendo around them. Clouds fell over the moon and blotted out the light.

"She's coming. Please, Kalliope, get me to sanctuary. You're his only hope."

Her heart dropped. "Who? Him who?" *Lugh!*

Shrieks filled the clearing. The water began to freeze over. Anubis stood up, but fell back down. From the boundaries of the forest, she saw a form. It had large wings, but there was no more to it. She couldn't make out any features. Her breath came out in fog. Cold crept around her legs, trying to pull her down. She grabbed the god's hand and hauled him toward the large oak tree. The bark was rough under her hand when it should have been soft. The screams were closer. Ice was forming in her hair.

"All ways are barred to me. No one will take me in or they face her wrath."

"Anubis, stop being so sour. Whoever is after you won't get you. I've held off a godly coup. I'm sure I can handle whoever is hunting you." She placed her hand on the bark again and concentrated on the beings inside. Dagda, Flidais, and even the chess-playing beaver stood near the wall of the tree. "Dadga, open up. I don't know what's going on here, but you can't leave me out in the cold. I'm practically family, and I've never known you to turn your back on another god. Let us in."

She pushed all her power into moving through the tree, but nothing was happening. The cold was near her. If she peeked behind her, the thing after Anubis would be there. She struggled not to glance back. Her hope was faltering. After everything, Dagda was going to abandon her and she didn't know where Lugh was. Cold breath puffed against the back of her neck. Something stood behind her. Whoever it was, they only had seconds left. The echoes of the shadows were a cacophony and deafened her. Kalliope dared a peek back, but a hand enclosed around her wrist and pulled her through the bark. The last thing she saw before the bark was a pair of deep red eyes. Once she and Anubis were through, she landed on her knees inside on a grass floor. When she looked up, it was into Flidais's troubled gaze.

Chapter Three

"Thanks for the rescue. It took you long enough." Kalliope accepted the hand and got up. She dusted herself off. Flidais stepped back while Kalliope helped Anubis to his feet. A shudder ran down her back from being in the warm environment. The image of those crimson eyes burned into her mind. She didn't know what the being was, but she would never forget those eyes. And the woman she had seen under the trees. She was another mystery. The howling continued outside the tree even though it was faint. All of a sudden, a face pressed up against the tree bark and screamed, trying to get in. It wasn't able to penetrate the inner sanctum of the oak tree. This was Dagda's lair, and nothing came in or out of it unless he said so. Anubis knelt before Dagda.

"Great Celtic Lord, I humbly request asylum."

Dagda sighed and glanced at Kalliope. "You certainly have gotten us into a pickle, haven't you? And I don't mean a dill one either."

She threw up her hands. "I didn't go looking for this, whatever this is. I wasn't loaned out either."

The god stroked his brown beard until it was shot through with green moss. "You won't ever let me live that down, will you?"

"No. Why do you think I haven't brought you any coffee? You keep it up, and you won't get any at the wedding."

The other god pouted. He ran and did cartwheels around the inside of the tree. Kalliope got dizzy watching him. *Just when I think I have him figured out, he goes and does something crazy. I think he's been locked up in this stupid tree for too long.*

Flidais shook her head. "Now you've gone and done it." She placed a hand on Anubis's shoulder. "Old friend, you are welcome here. Nothing will harm you. You may claim haven for as long as you need it."

The death god was relieved. He stood, picked Flidais up, and spun her around. She squealed and then he set her down again. "It has been too long, Lid. Why haven't you come to the tombs to say hello? The sphinx and the other gods get so dry. The only refuge I get is playing poker with David. Now and again, my warriors make me laugh, but they are really hard core."

"I've been a little busy helping Kalliope plan a wedding and spending time with Dagda. Did you know that I was *human* for a year?" Flidais giggled.

Anubis's golden eyes widened. "Why would you become one of those sniveling simpletons?"

Kalliope didn't appreciate the tone of his voice. "Hey, bub. Remember who saved your ass just a minute ago. Flidais, I'm sorry to interrupt your reunion and all, but I need to know what the hell just happened. Anubis, who attacked you? Who were the other gods you were with? What have I gotten myself involved with now?"

The Egyptian god growled and showed his curved teeth. "It's Isis. She's gone off her obelisk. We all know she's been pining for Osiris for centuries. After his death and her failed resurrection attempt, she and I started seeing one another. We've been off and on again forever, but this last time we broke up, something was different. I thought she would be okay, but this time, she's sent Ammut after me to swallow my essence, my power. I assume it's her way of trying to get back at me. The she-demon struck me in the back with a cursed dagger when I was at Lugh's bachelor party. She got some of the other gods too."

"Is Lugh okay?" Her breath caught in her throat. Nothing bad could have happened to him. If it had, she would have known. If he died, so would she.

"I honestly don't know. I heard the screams of the ka, the lost souls, and knew Ammut was coming. I tried to warn the others, but they were all too drunk on ambrosia. The she-demon won't stop until I'm devoured and Isis is happy. I had nowhere else to go. Forgive me for dragging you into this, Kalliope, but I didn't know who else would help. The news of your impending marriage and what you did for All Hail last year is still the talk of the Underworlds. I was counting on you to assist me." The jackal took her hand and brushed a kiss over her knuckles.

Kalliope quivered. His breath smelled of rot. *This is all I need. Now I've become the superhero of the gods. I have a life besides saving their supernatural asses. Lugh! Where are you?* Tears spilled down her cheeks. She needed space. Her heart throbbed against her chest. Her emotions threatened to overwhelm her reason, and she wasn't sure exactly what she was going to do. Part of her wanted to lash out and do some serious harm to Anubis for involving her in yet another mystical adventure. The other part yearned to have Lugh in her arms so that she could feel every part of him to make sure he wasn't injured. After walking away, she slid down the wall of the oak tree and pressed her face against her knees. *Gotta get a hold of myself. I can do this.* She took in a breath and focused on Lugh. Love was the strongest magick in the world. It bridged great distances and dimensions.

She calmed herself enough and envisioned her love. How soft his hands were. The touch of his lips on her throat. How good they fit together. The way he smelled of pine and musk. He was the sun, and she the flower that turned its face to him. Together, they had a bond that nothing could break, not even death. Her inner sense carried her along their connection until she found herself standing in the middle of a failed bachelor party. Bodies littered the ground. There were at least twenty gods all passed out with no visible wounds. Lugh was among them on a sumptuous lip-shaped sofa. He wore a purple leather thong, had lipstick prints all over his face and chest, and his toenails were painted pink. She even noticed lipstick marks on the thong right over his package. A wave of irritation went through her. He wouldn't cheat on her, even though in the past he was known for being a womanizer. He had a pink garter on his well-muscled left thigh. She couldn't help it and ran her tongue along his chest. Even though her astral self was invisible, he could still feel her presence. She tasted honey on the tip of her tongue. Lugh stirred more when she nipped his neck. He opened his eyes when she tickled under his knee.

Lugh put a hand to his head. "Oh, remind me never again to drink ambrosia and elderberry wine mixed together. Kalliope, love, what's going on?" he asked while surveying the other gods.

She chuckled, having never seen him with a hangover before. *"You were attacked. Anubis said some demon was set on him. He showed up at the shop with a dagger in his back. Anubis asked for sanctuary, and I really couldn't say no. Now I'm with Dagda wondering if you're okay. I think I got myself into the middle of something. Are you okay?"*

He touched her cheek. "I'm fine, love. You know now that you're involved, you can't just back away from this."

"I know. Universal Law, yadayada. Been there before. Really don't want to do it again, but whatever. Get your ass over here now. I want to feel every inch of you to make sure you're really okay."

He gave her a wide, playful smile. "Every inch of me?"

"Yes. Just make sure you get rid of the thong. I don't need anyone else's lip prints on what is rightfully mine."

"You know I didn't do anything to—"

She summoned her power and sent a blast of cold along their tie. He curled his fists and drew in a breath. "Oh god, that makes me so hot. I want to spirit you away and show you some of the wonderful tricks I've learned from the other gods."

Kalliope experienced the echo of his pleasure and envisioned pinching his rounded butt. He jumped. *"I'd love to right now. And I know you didn't do anything. A girl can get a little jealous once in awhile. Besides, I don't want you to forget about what I can do to you."*

He laughed. "If I were there right now and didn't feel like I'd been bowled over by a score of chariots, I'd make you regret those words."

"Well then get your butt better and get over here. Are the rest of them going to be okay?"

"I think so. I'll wake them up and then come for you. Wear something tight with leather."

She raised her eyebrows. He had never made requests before. *This could be fun. We'll see.* She brushed her lips against his cheek and willed herself back to her body. Her limbs were numb from her being gone so long. When she lifted her head, the room was spinning. All the gods were staring at her.

"Everything okay?" Flidais asked.

She nodded. "Yeah, it appears Lugh and the other gods were passed out cold. I had to warm Lugh up to get him to come around. He'll be here soon."

The goddess nodded.

"So, what happens now? Do we just wait and see what happens with Anubis? Do we go to Isis and plead our case?"

The fairies inside the oak tree dive bombed her. The first one hit her side and bounced off. She hated the little things. Kalliope reached down, grabbed the fairy by its bushy squirrel tail, and held it up before her. It was a miniature person with small pointed ears, iridescent wings, and wearing a pink dress. It glared at her and shook its fist and squirmed around. She couldn't understand its high-pitched voice, but she knew it wanted to be let go. "I let you go, you and your little friends leave me alone, deal?"

The fairy hung limp in her fingers and drummed her fingers on her chin. She screwed up her face and then said something to Kalliope. She glanced at Flidais. "What did she say?"

The goddess laughed. "Lucidria said that the only way she'd do whatever you wanted is if you offered her the one thing that she wants."

"What does she want?"

"She wants a date with Dustbunny. She said if you can accomplish that, she'll be forever in your debt and won't even think about crashing your wedding like they had all planned on."

Kalliope glanced at the fairy who was giving her the evil eye. The little creature's arms were folded over her chest and she was waiting. *How can a fairy and a goblin date? The logistics of it don't make any sense.* She wasn't sure how she was going to get the goblin to go out with the fairy. At least he was more reasonable than his brother, Ickleberry, the goblin that used to be her roommate. She shivered thinking about all the mornings he had woke her up at six, jostling her pots and pans around. There were so many times she'd wanted to kill him. "Fine. I'll see what I can do, but you owe me more than not crashing my wedding. How will I know if you'll keep your bargain?"

She made more squeaking sounds and poked her. Kalliope glanced at the goddess for translation.

"She says, unlike humans, fairies keep their word. Once you get her a date, you…" Flidais stopped and stared at the fairy. "Are you sure?" Lucidria made more sounds. "She said that once you get her a date, you'll be part of the colony. Extended family. Fairies don't do that often."

Kalliope let the twittering fairy go. She hovered before her face and waited for an answer. *Great. Even more stuff I have to do. How in the world do I get involved with these things? Sometimes, I wish I'd never eaten those apples. Of course then I'd never have gotten involved with Lugh and I'd probably be Cromm's love slave.*

She glanced at Anubis, who was staring at the wall of the tree. The screams of the ka were no longer audible, but something pressed its face against the bark, still trying to break in. The wall kept changing scenery, so whatever was out there was stuck in the bark. The impending doom of the mission ahead loomed over her. Now that she'd become involved, there was nothing to stop it. She'd bound herself by Universal Law to assist the god. Kalliope hoped it wasn't the same with the fairy.

"Fine. I'll ask him, but can you make me understand you? For some reason, my magick isn't working on you, and you sound like fingernails on a chalkboard. That is so not a way to communicate."

The fairy did the *I Dream of Jeannie* arms crossed and head bob. "Is that better?" Her smile spread on her little face, and Kalliope assumed what she did was just for showing off.

"Wonderful. Thanks. No fairy dust to go along with that?" Kalliope muttered.

"I don't do *sparkly*." Her eyes narrowed. "You have a thing with that, mortal?"

"I was just saying. Being fairies, you think the glitter and bubbles would be raining down by now."

The fairy raged and flew back into the lily chandelier above. Kalliope glanced at Flidais, who had a disappointed expression on her face.

"You could've been nicer to Lucidria. She is the fairy queen and all."

Kalliope walked past the goddess. She was antsy all of a sudden. "Sorry. I didn't see the crown."

"What's gotten into you?" Flidais inquired.

She shrugged and ran a hand through her scarlet locks. "Nothing. I'm just tired. You know, pre-wedding jitters and all. I haven't been getting my beauty rest. I'll be fine." *Will I really be fine?* Things were happening so fast. She needed Lugh to steady her. *I need for all of this supernatural crap to end. Now I'm a matchmaker.*

"Dagda, Flidais, I need your help." Lugh materialized out of nowhere carrying a limp David, cheesecake god extraordinaire. Dagda reappeared and rushed over to Lugh. They placed the inert cheesecake god on a sofa that grew out of the bottom of the floor from vines and flowers, quickly weaving itself into furniture.

"What happened?" Kalliope asked, peering over everyone's shoulders. She saw her fiancé's troubled gaze. It was very unlike him to be so anxious.

"I was able to revive the others, but he hasn't come around. I don't sense his life force or his power. He's hollow."

Dagda pushed his grandson out of the way. When he did, his clothes changed to a doctor's lab coat and he listened to David's heart with a stethoscope. After a moment, he raised his head. "I'm afraid he's gone. Nurse, get me a crash cart."

Fliadais nudged him in the ribs. "Dagda, take this seriously. What would the world do without cheesecake?" She placed one hand on David's head and one over his heart and closed her eyes. When she opened them, there were tears on her lashes. "He's gone. Who could do such a thing? I've never heard of this before. Who could drain a god's power?"

"It was Ammut. She's the only one who can devour the essences of gods."

"But why would anyone want to hurt David? What did he do besides win an ungodly amount of money at poker? Make someone the wrong kind of cheesecake?" Kalliope queried.

"I don't know why, but David never cheated. He loses most hands to let us win. I do know that the only one who can give him his soul back is Ammut, and she'll only do that if Ma'at orders it. And the only one to command Ma'at is Isis."

Kalliope rolled her eyes. Now she had to face the goddess on two fronts. One to see if she passed whatever test the goddess had up her sleeve about her being together with Lugh, and then to plead her case for David and Anubis. "Great. So what pyramid or obelisk does she live in? Hopefully, we can have this all sorted out before anyone can say King Tut and then I can get back to my wedding plans."

"King Tut!" Dagda chimed in.

"Can't you do something about him?" Kalliope asked Flidais. She was seriously getting tired of the ruler of the Celtic gods acting so childish. The whole carnival sideshow act was getting old. Dagda was only doing it because he could. Underneath all his antics, he was a serious man that could smite her with a look if he wanted.

"No one has to do anything about me, sweet Kalli. I can take care of myself. Now you will help Anubis get those banshees off him and stop pressing against my tree and find David's essence before all the factories of cheesecake wink out and your mortal world forgets the decadent dessert that cheesecake really is?"

"Is that an order? Because I paid my debt to you when you sent me to Zeus. I saved the world once already. I'm not doing this!" Kalliope summoned her magick and wanted to be far away from everyone. She didn't care where she was going. It had to be where there were no people. Just silence so she could have time to think.

Lugh gazed at her with an odd expression. He tried to caress her, but before his touch reached her, she winked out.

Chapter Four

Kalliope reappeared and landed on her butt. Her head spun, and it took her a few moments to get her bearings. Before her were endless rolling hills and green grass. The whistling wind and the rustle of the blades were the only sounds. She shivered when the wind tickled over her flesh. Picturing herself in jeans and a T-shirt, she wanted to be clad in a little something more protective, but when she reached for her power, there was nothing. *What the heck is going on?* She glanced up. The sun was setting at the edge of the horizon, splashing apricots and yellows through the sky.

"Well, I wanted to get away from it all." She sighed. The breeze picked up and blew her hair into her face. She pushed it out of the way and noticed that her engagement ring was gone. When she studied her other fingers, the ring that Nas had given her last year was also gone. Both of the rings shouldn't have been able to come off. *How in the world did this happen? Where the hell am I? What happened to me? Why don't I have my magick?* Her hand flew to her throat. She was even without the silver pentacle that Flidais had given her. Everything that was related to the gods had disappeared from her being. The gust kicked up again, and she sneezed. She hadn't done that since she had been struck by Cupid's lust arrow last year and had an allergic reaction. Come to think of it, she hadn't had any allergic reactions or gotten sick since she'd gotten her magick.

"Dagda, if you blinked me somewhere to make me learn a lesson, then very funny. Bring me back, please. Taking away the things that Nas and Flidais gave me, okay, but you can't have my engagement ring. Come on. I'm sorry. I was frustrated with you. I had a bad day. A girl's entitled to those every once in awhile," Kalliope yelled to the empty air. She didn't get a response. *What am I going to do? Well, standing here certainly isn't going to do me any good. There has to be someone around here.*

She kept on going toward the setting sun, heading west. After walking for hours, watching the sun sink lower behind the mountains, she was getting nowhere. She came upon a small pond. Gratefully, she sank down next to it and scooped up handfuls of water. The liquid was cold and quenched her thirst, but it didn't do anything for the empty feeling in her gut. She glanced at her hand again, feeling the absence of Lugh's ring. The darkness was chilly and she couldn't read the stars above. *I should've paid more attention when Morgaine was teaching me astrology last year.* All the walking had given her time to think. Her stomach rumbled, but food was the last thing on her mind. She was more worried about Lugh.

After drinking, she gazed into the pool, longing to get a glimpse of her beloved. Even after everything she'd gone through since she'd met him, she wouldn't give up the times she had with him. He often joked with her that she was born from one of his solar flares, which was why they fit so perfectly together. She was just so tired of the shenanigans and goings on of the other gods and the magick world. Sometimes, she wished Lugh were human and they had the perfect white picket fence and two point five children.

She closed her eyes and reached down inside of her. She might not have the ring he'd given her, but his love remained. They couldn't do anything to block that. Kalliope concentrated, and sensed the link between the two of them. When she touched upon it, warmth flared through her. Tears dotted her eyes. She tried sending her love along their connection, but it was blocked.

"Why can't life be simpler? I didn't ask to be cut off from anyone."

"Is that what you truly wish?"

Kalliope jumped and saw Lugh sitting only inches from her. She reached out to him, but was met with an invisible barrier so she couldn't touch him. She tried again, but couldn't get through it. Gazing into his eyes, she saw the most forlorn expression she'd ever seen on him. "I don't know," she admitted. "All the magick stuff is great, but I just want you. What happened to me? Why don't I have your ring? Did I do something wrong?"

"You're having second thoughts now that you've lived in my world and know the consequences of it. I can bestow upon you the gift that you seek—that you'd never been touched by magick. Of course you would forget about me. You'd live out your days happy and blissful. I'd look down on you every day while the sun shines, watching you grow old and eventually die. In the old days, it was tricky for mortals and gods to consort with one another. That was one reason why All Hail decreed magick should be banished. That and we gods found it difficult to lose the humans we loved. Some were exalted and became gods themselves. Tell me what you want and I'll grant it. I can't give you a mixture. It must be one or the other. I took anything that would remind you of the gods because, deep down, we both know the answer."

She shook her head. Tears stung her eyes. *This isn't happening. He's saying he loves me, but he'll let me go because I want to be human. Lugh would never say that to me. He just wouldn't.* She didn't know how to answer him. "I don't know. I can't lose you. This isn't right. Just because I'm thinking of something doesn't mean. I—"

He brushed her forehead with his lips. "You don't have to say anything. I've already read your heart. I'll always love you, Kalli. No matter what happens."

A tingling sensation started in her forehead and began to trickle through her. She tried to hold onto Lugh, but the more she tried, the tougher it was. He became transparent and then faded out completely. Her head spun and before she knew it, she collapsed.

* * * *

"Miss? Miss, are you okay?"

Kalliope opened her eyes. Her head throbbed and it felt like she was hung over. Standing before her was an olive-skinned man with a black beard and black hair. The man offered her his hand. She took it gratefully and got up. When she glanced down at her clothes, she was in a white sheer dress. The way the man leered at her, she knew he saw everything. Uncomfortable in the situation, she crossed her arms over her breasts, trying to hide them.

"Are you okay?" he asked her again.

She took in the enormous dunes that rolled and dipped off into the distance. The vast emptiness reflected the hollow ache she had inside of her. The landscape around her was nothing more than sand. Tons and tons of sand. *How in the world did I get here? The last thing I remember...* She thought back. *I don't know what the last thing I remember is. Crap. That isn't good.* "I don't know if I'm okay." She scratched her head and realized there was lot of sand in her hair.

"How did you get here?"

She spun around again, trying to get her bearings. Nothing was coming to mind. She glanced at her hands and saw they were bare, but on her left hand was the impression of a ring. Something that she had worn for a long time because the indentation in her skin was deep. "I don't know. Where is here?" *I wonder if I was engaged? Did I lose the ring?* Kalliope thought about it and she didn't feel like she'd broken up with someone. A feeling of love so strong swept through her that it took her breath away. *Wow. Whatever that was it means that I gotta be connected to someone and that he's looking for me.*

"You're in the middle of the Sahara Desert. Jack and I were on our way to Cairo. Maybe someone there can help you. Come. I am Abbas."

"Who's Jack?" she asked. She had no other place to go, so Cairo it was.

Her guide smiled. "Jack is my camel." He walked a few steps and patted the largest camel she had ever seen.

Jack was lying down. He had a saddle between his humps that had things dangling from it. The smell coming off him was overpowering. She pressed her hand over her nose to keep from gagging. Her guide took out a bottle, brought it to his lips, and then handed it to her. "Drink a little. Water will help you."

She did what she was told and drank a couple of swallows. The water wasn't cold, but it was refreshing. It made her realize how parched her throat was. Licking her lips, she noticed they were dry and cracked. Abbas dug into one of his packs and handed her a long blue cloth. "Thanks. What's this for?"

Her guide rolled his eyes. "Put it on your head and wrap it around your face. It will help with the sun and keep out the sand. Come on. We are wasting time." He motioned her to get on the camel. Kalliope eyed the beast. She sensed Jack and she weren't going to get along. The camel let out a long grunt, raised its lip in a sneer, and then spit at her. It landed all over her dress.

"Ick!" She began dabbing at it with the cloth her rescuer had given her.

"That only means he likes you. Come on."

"Likes me. Gee, what does he do if he loves me?" Kalliope wrapped the scarf around her head and mouth and then climbed onto the camel. Instantly, she regretted that she was wearing a dress. The coarse camel hairs scratched her inner thighs. She began wriggling. Her guide didn't seem to notice, but got on in front of her. They got on their way and she tried to hold onto the hump before her, but ended up grabbing onto her guide's waist.

He glanced behind him and gave her a wide grin. She forced a smile and pulled away. She squirmed, trying to ignore the itching. The hair was poking into her skin, but she just kept on shimmying on the camel's back, trying to pay no attention to the itching. No matter how much she adjusted her dress or scratched the enflamed area, it wasn't doing any good. Throughout their trek, her thighs began to burn. The one good thing was that it took her mind off of trying to remember who she was and where she had come from. Sitting on her hands didn't do any good. It only made it worse. The sweltering sun beat down on her so she was overheated in the scarf and sweating rivers.

After what seemed like hours, the sandy landscape changed. On the horizon she saw a sparkling blue river and a large triangle reaching toward the sky. Those were pyramids. How she knew that, she wasn't sure. Just that they were. She knew the names of things, but when it came to thinking about her life and her past, she wasn't able to recall anything. Her guide stopped on the outskirts of a small town. *Civilization. Maybe I can use a phone and…no, that won't do me any good because I don't know anyone's number. Damnit.* He helped her down from Jack, but she could barely walk due to the welts on her legs and thighs.

"Come. My wife will be able to help you." Abbas motioned her inside. She glanced around her at the square mud houses and then back at the camel. Jack had an evil gleam in his eye. She trusted her guide more than she did the pack animal.

"Great," she muttered. She ambled along, trying to keep her thighs from rubbing together and making the rash worse, but it wasn't going so well. They entered the sparsely furnished house, and a small woman with nice features and a smile came out. Her dark brown eyes widened when she saw Kalliope. Her black hair was pulled away from her face in a ponytail. She reminded her of a bird because she was so petite.

"Hi!" Kalliope squeaked.

The woman nodded and nothing else. Her guide and his wife said something in Arabic. Her guide kept pointing at her, and his wife would glance over but never make eye contact. Kalliope wasn't sure how to react. The last thing she wanted to do was offend anyone. So she stood and took in the house. A few photographs of the family lined the wall. A small table was piled high with books. A black futon was pushed against the wall.

"My wife will help you. She understands English pretty well, but doesn't speak it as well. I must go. Maybe you will be able to remember more about how you ended up in the middle of the desert."

"Thanks, Abbas." Kalliope watched him leave and she sat down on the futon, glad that it wasn't on four legs or swaying. After a moment, his wife came out with a bowl of water and a cloth. She took the cloth and wiped Kalliope's legs. Her hands traveled up her thighs, and Kalliope jumped back to awareness.

"Whoa!"

The woman stopped. "It will help." She gestured to the welts.

Kalliope took the cloth and smelled something sweet on it. It was also coming from the water. She placed the wet cloth against her legs and watched the red welts begin to shrink. Dabbing more liquid on them, the hives began to heal. Nothing could make someone heal so fast. Something wasn't normal about the water. Her instincts dinged that she should know something was going on around her, but she couldn't figure out what it was. She pressed the cloth to her forehead and the smell relaxed her.

"Thanks. What's your name?"

The woman cocked her head. After a moment, she responded. "Corrine. You?"

"Corrine. That's a nice name. Me? I think it's Kalli." She traced the indentation from the ring and felt the warmth rush through her almost as if it were reassuring her she wasn't alone. She wasn't able to recall anything no matter how much she tried. All she wanted was an image of the man who went with the feeling. Sighing, she kept dabbing the water on her legs to make the rash go away. *I'll never get on a camel again. At least not while I'm wearing a dress.*

"Eat?" Corrine motioned toward her mouth. Kalliope figured she was asking if she was hungry. She thought about it and realized that she was.

"Yeah. Thanks."

Corrine smiled and went into the kitchen. After a few minutes, she came back out with a plate of bread and figs. Kalliope accepted the plate and began to nibble on the contents. While she was eating, she had a craving for something sweeter. Something cold. She licked her lips at the thought of ice cream.

"Thank you. Here." She offered the plate to Corrine, who waved her off. Kalliope finished, and even though she was full, she felt empty. Not being able to remember anything was disheartening. *What is going on with me? Why am I in the middle of the desert dressed like I was going to a toga party? It's really sad I can't remember what my favorite food is.* She wiped her eyes from the tears.

"Don't cry. Things will be okay."

Kalliope wiped her eyes. Another woman stood in the doorway with a dark scarf covering most of her face. Her dark eyes bored into Kalliope's, but she dropped her gaze. Corrine began to shout at the woman. The one in the scarf replied and then waved her hand. At once, her hostess was hurled back against the wall and knocked out. Kalliope was stunned and shrank from the woman. *That's not possible. She didn't even touch Corrine. What's going on here? None of this is natural.* She backed away slowly toward the fallen woman.

"What did you do to her?"

The woman chuckled. "Nothing you need to worry about. Come with me, Kalliope. I'll bring you back so that you know what happened. Of course it would only prove what I've said all along. Don't you want to make all of this go away?" She extended her hand. Kalliope noticed her nails were painted deep purple with gold tips.

Kalliope. That's my name. It rang a bell. She glanced between the woman and Corrine, but retreated. Something wasn't right. "I'm not going anywhere with you."

She gathered Corrine up in her arms and tried to rouse her. Her head lolled on her knee, leaving a streak of blood on her white dress. Corrine had hit the wall harder than she thought. Snatching the rag she had used on her leg, she pressed it against the wound, hoping whatever healing powers it had would work for Corrine. *I have to get her to a doctor.*

"If you don't come with me, then you won't ever get back what you've lost. Don't you want to remember where you came from? I can give you all the answers. I can even give you back the ring you've been wondering about. Look familiar?" She closed her fist, and when she opened it, there was a red diamond ring in her palm. Seeing it tugged a familiar chord inside her.

"Where did you get that?"

A wicked gleam came to her eye. "I was the one who took them in the first place. Here. As a show of good faith." She threw the ring.

Kalliope went to catch it, but couldn't. However, she felt the weight on her finger. Glancing down, she saw that the ring was in the same exact spot where the indentation had been. *Who is this woman? What other things did she take from me? Was she the one who put me in the middle of the desert?*

"I haven't got all day. A simple yes will do."

Kalliope gazed between it and the woman in her arms. She couldn't leave Corrine alone. She wasn't heartless. Even though she was being offered the chance to regain her memory, she wasn't about to run off when someone was helpless and wounded. "No, sorry. I wouldn't go with you even if you presented me the world. Not after what you did to Corrine. I can't leave her hurt and alone. It would be inhumane."

The woman shrugged. "Suit yourself, but if you don't come with me, you'll suffer the consequences. You may never know who gave you that ring or who you really are."

Consequences? If I go with her, this crazy nightmare will be over. No, I can't do that. She stared at the woman and noticed at the window observing them was another woman similarly dressed in a black outfit with a veil covering her face. She stuck her chin out. "I can't leave her injured like this. Even if it costs me my memory." She pressed the cloth more to Corrine's head, hoping the bleeding had stopped. After a moment, she heard screaming. When she looked up again, Abbas stood in the doorway and both women were gone. He yelled something at her she didn't understand and pointed. He rushed in and snatched his wife from her hands.

"What have you done to her?"

"I didn't do anything. I swear. There was another woman here. She threw her against the wall."

"I don't believe you. I knew it was bad luck to bring you here. I never should've listened to that woman who told me to head out into the sand. Finding gold, my ass. Get out! I knew it was a bad omen."

Kalliope shrunk back and left the house. All the commotion had attracted a mob. She began to push through the group of men when Abbas came out and began telling the people what she had done both in English and his native tongue. The crowd grew larger, but she wasn't able to escape them. Someone grabbed her and dragged her toward the center of town.

"She's a witch. She did something to Corrine. Now she has to pay," Abbas accused her. The other members of town roared. She struggled and tried to get away from the men holding her. They tightened their grips on her arms. She studied the hungry expressions on their faces. Her dress was really a bad idea.

"I'm not a witch. I didn't do anything. Please. It was someone else."

"Why should we believe you? You were the only one in the house. You're a stranger here. You were out in the desert alone with no water or provisions. You must have been put there for a reason."

"I don't know why. I can't remember. Please!" She saw a woman in the background. "There she is. That was the woman who hurt your wife." She pointed toward the woman in black. Some followed her outstretched hand and others didn't.

"There's no one there. She's trying to trick us," Abbas said.

"We have to take care of her before anyone from outside the village gets wind that she was ever here."

One of the men holding her said, "Let me take her. She's a pretty one. We could use a serving wench. Or better yet, my son needs another wife."

"You can't. I'm engaged to someone."

The man laughed. "If someone loved you so much then where is he? Did you kill him too?"

There were a few more words said around her, but she didn't understand them. When she met the woman's gaze in the distance, she saw nothing but judgment. No one was going to help her. Kalliope didn't know what to do. Frantically, she tried to pull away from her captors. They had more than lust in their eyes. They had murder in them. While she struggled, something struck her arm. Before she registered the pain, another object hit her leg. Then one on her chest. At that point, the men weren't holding her. She stumbled and realized that the throng was throwing stones at her. Another rock hit the side of her face. The impact forced her to wiggle her jaw a couple of times to make sure it wasn't broken.

This can't be happening to me. I don't even know how I got here. Who I am. I didn't do this. I didn't. Why is this happening to me? "Please, you don't understand—" she protested, but another rock whacked her square on the chest this time. She stumbled backward from the onslaught to protect her face. Her butt hit something steady. The horde advanced, pelting her with rocks and bits of whatever they could find. Through her crossed arms, she could see the woman in black just beyond the multitude waiting to see what would happen to her. She tried to back up more, but felt another hard hit on her head. Stunned, she fell backward from the impact.

All she knew was that she was falling. The air ballooned around her. For a moment, the cushion of air felt wonderful, and then she hit. There was a loud sound and then agonizing sting where her back slammed into the water. Her eyes were open; the breath was knocked out of her, and she sunk to the bottom.

Chapter Five

The water surrounded her on all sides. She couldn't breathe. Her life, what little she remembered of it, flashed before her eyes. Kalliope struggled to remember to swim. Her limbs hurt. Her head ached from where she had been pummeled. All she wanted to do was give up, but something inside of her couldn't. The thought of the person who gave her the ring kept her going. That feeling of warmth she had before overcame her. Something snapped inside of her, and she swam her way to the surface. At once, her lungs drank in the cool, life-giving air. She wiped the water from her eyes, stared up the long, dark tunnel, and saw tiny faces peering down at her. More uproar echoed down around her. A large bucket sat a few feet up, dangling by a rope. She tried to grab it, but no matter how much she stretched her fingertips, it was just out of reach. She swam over to the side of the well to get her bearings. Her heard hurt, but she had to concentrate through the pain and think of a way to get out.

The interior of the well was smooth with no place to grab a hold of to climb up. *Even if I did make it back up, I don't want to face the angry mob again. Great. I'm stuck down here.* She sighed and then noticed that one part of the wall was sunken in. *Maybe. Just maybe.* Swimming over to it, she touched the hole. Sand and rock gave way around the opening. She scooped more out, noticing it was easy going. After a few more key rocks, the hole opened up completely.

The only way is to find something at the end of this tunnel. Please let there be something at the end. She took a deep breath and hopped into the passageway. *At least it's dry*. It was completely dark, so she wasn't able to see anything, just feel her way around her.

Kalliope heard things moving around in the tunnel with her. Her fingers sunk into dry sand in some places. In others, it was stone. A couple of times when she put her hand in the sand, something darted out from underneath her palms. The narrow space began to get to her. She had to stop and take a few deep breaths to remind herself this was the only way she could go. At first she was on her hands and knees, scraping the skin on her legs, and tearing her dress to shreds. After awhile, the tunnel shrunk so she had to shimmy through on her stomach and pull herself along. Her legs were raw, and her palms stung each time she moved through the earth, but the farther she got, the more she heard a roar. It was faint at first. The air was getting stale and she was growing lightheaded. She had to get to the end soon before she ran out of breathable air.

Tarrying onward, the thundering got louder until she pushed out to the end of the channel. It was a struggle because she had to twist around to get her head out of the opening and then her shoulders. When she was out, she emerged into a large cavern. It wasn't pitch black due to a few shafts of sunlight shining down from above her and reflecting off the walls. In the middle of the grotto was a rushing river. The sun caught crystals in the earth, and prisms of rainbows bounced around the cave walls. She pulled herself from the hole and walked toward the water. There was a fast current, but she was able to splash some water on her face and clean off some of the dirt and grime that she had on her.

She sipped some of the water and saw there was a definite diagonal pattern to the beams of sunlight. Walking toward one of them, she touched the wall where it reflected. A large amount of sand fell to the floor. The beam of light increased. She noticed the shiny metal on the wall. *Wow, these must be some ancient mirrors.* Upon further investigation, she discovered writing on the cave walls. *These are hieroglyphics. Maybe I'm under some ancient pyramid. I'm surprised that the others in the village never found this.*

With her curiosity piqued, she decided to follow the sunlight beam down the tunnel. *All I have is time to kill. Maybe I'll come upon some prehistoric city or something where mole people dwell. It's better than going back up the well and facing the irate horde.*

She followed the bouncing sunlight further along the side of the rushing river. She'd stop once in awhile and saw that she was actually following a path that probably hadn't been used in thousands of years. She made out more hieroglyphics along the walls, but had no idea what they said. They kept depicting a creature with the body of a man and the head of a dog. *No, not a dog. A jackal.*

At the end of the passageway, the river disappeared underneath a large stone wall. However, a mirror shone on a blocked stone barricade. Kalliope ran her hands over the partition, wiping away the dust and caked sand. The image of a large sun and an ankh was carved into the door. She wiped more of it off and uncovered pictures of people bowing down before the large jackal creature again. On closer inspection, something moved underneath her hand. There was a click. The wall shook as more sand showered around her. She jumped back in time to see the wall swing open. Once that happened, the sunlight caught another mirror, and the passageway before her was lit.

Curtains of cobwebs lay before her all with dozens of various sizes of spiders nesting in the middle of them.

Great. I get to go down there. I hate spiders. Or do I? I don't know, but those suckers look nasty. She glanced behind her and wasn't sure if she headed back if she would even find her way out of the underground corridors she was in. *I wish I had some fire to ward these things off.* Ancient torches lined the wall, sitting in their holders, but they didn't pop on for her. *Great.*

She took a deep breath and pushed through the first cobweb. The spider didn't seem disturbed, and besides being wrapped up like a mummy in the webbing, she was fine. Kalliope pressed on, passing through the webs and ignoring the accusing stares of the domed-eyed arachnids.

Halfway down the hallway, she was met with the mother of all spiders. It was bad enough she was getting the creepy crawlies and felt the eight-legged beasts crawling on her when there weren't any, but the one in front of her wasn't moving. It was at least three feet across and a foot wide. Its eyes were trained on her. She heard scurrying behind her. When she looked back, the spiders she'd avoided were creeping toward her.

Her heart picked up speed and sweat beaded on her forward. "Ahh, hi! Any way you would want to move to let me pass?" she asked the spider. The spider's fangs clapped together. It glided down its web so it was eye level with her. Kalliope peered into its twelve round eyes that reminded her of black, glossy marbles. She felt the presence of the other spiders behind her, but didn't dare peek back to see if the daddy was leading the pack, because it might be as big as the mommy spider before her.

The spider studied her for a long time. The only noise was the soft patter of the spiders behind her in the sand. In the spider's eyes, she saw herself. The tense, fearful expression on her face. The short, quick breaths she was taking in. And the blanket of spiders covering the walls and ceiling behind her.

"Why should we let you pass when you're trespassing upon this sacred ground?"

It took Kalliope a moment to realize the spider had spoken. *Okay, this is* not *normal.* "Ahh…I'm sorry. I didn't know this was consecrated ground. I-I'm kinda lost. If you can tell me how to get out of here, I'll certainly get out of your hair."

"You destroyed my children's webs. For that, you should pay. My spiderlings have not eaten well in a long time. You'd make them an exceptional meal. But I'll let you pass if you do something for me."

"Sure, whatever you want." She really didn't feel like being the main course for a few dozen spiders. Whatever the task was, she was going to jump on it.

"You must take me beyond this passageway and deeper into the temple. I must find out what has happened to our master. I am barred from going beyond this corridor. I am its guardian."

Kalliope shivered at the thought of going along with the spider, but if it knew a way out, then she would help it out. Part of her wasn't past the idea she was talking to and understanding the large arachnid. "I can use the company, so sure."

The spider made a large hissing noise she figured was laughter. There was a tickling along her feet. She glanced down and saw that the little spiders were now creeping all over her toes. She didn't dare move in case she squashed one of them. If she did that, she figured she would be in deep crap. Or if they decided to bite her and they were all poisonous, she was doomed.

"It isn't that simple, human. You must carry me through the barriers. Only a mortal can walk through them. Do you accept? Or will my spiderlings make you into their next meal? I can assure you it will be a slow death. My offspring know how to savor their food." The spider crossed its two front legs and waited.

Kalliope didn't have much of an option. The thought of the spider being near her was heart-stopping. She wasn't about to get wrapped up in a web and be the main course for the others either. "I don't intend on staying here that long. So hop on board."

The spider examined her then clapped her fangs together. The other spiders along her feet retreated, which made her relax some. The momma spider slid down from her web and skittered behind Kalliope. She didn't dare move when the spider climbed up her legs and then onto her back. It took all of her strength not to cry out. Her body shook uncontrollably while the spider cinched its eight legs around her stomach and its head lay on her shoulder. The spider didn't weigh more than a few pounds, but even the thought of it made her quiver. *Once this is all over, I never want to see another spider ever again.*

She walked through the passageway, trying to disregard the large arachnid on her back, but its hot breath blasted against her neck and made her shiver. The tough hairs on the spider's legs poked through her thin dress. Thankfully, the light of the sun was still beaming through the halls and reflecting off the mirrors. However, it wasn't as bright as it was before. That only meant that the sun was setting, and soon it would be dark. Once that happened, she didn't know what other beings would come out of the walls. Or if the spider would go back on its word and try and eat her.

The tunnel was filled with depictions of the jackal creature she had seen on the door. Figures were bowing to him. There were also images of ankhs and a setting sun. She saw some of a woman with large, outstretched wings. Everywhere Kalliope saw the image of the woman, she thought the woman's eyes leered at her. The vivid images were still vibrant. She stopped and ran her hand over the people, feeling the smooth paint underneath. She almost expected it to be wet. The paintings were so fresh they appeared alive.

"Those show how humans have worshipped my master for centuries. I remember when the priests painted these. It seems like yesterday," the spider reminisced.

Kalliope wondered how old the spider was. "Can I ask you something?"

"Anything but my age."

She laughed. *Just like any woman.* "Okay then. What's your name?"

"Ginger. And yours?"

"Kalliope. At least that's what I was told. I don't remember anything else."

"I bet it was her."

Kalliope heard the bitterness in the spider's voice. "Who her?"

"Never mind. It's not important, but I figure if she's out and about, then she must be behind the disappearance of my master."

"Well, no matter what's going on, have you thought how strange it is that I can understand you? I don't think that I go around talking to spiders every day. From what I can tell, no person has set foot down here in ages. When was the last time you had any visitors?"

The clapping of the spiders fangs sounded next to her ear. "A long time. And no, I don't know why you can understand me. Long ago, priests and priestesses used to worship me alongside the great Isis and Osiris. He was a wonderful specimen. So was his son. But I haven't had homage paid to me in a long time. I remember the sounds of the grinding when they placed the stone and blocked the entrance. They left several slaves for me and my family to feed from, but they were gone in a few months. Ever since then we've been fending for ourselves. My children bring me treats down from the world of men, but it has been a long time since I have ventured to the surface. They are allowed to travel all over this vast temple. I have been trapped on this level for a long time. My spiderlings have told me about the disturbances below. They heard the screams first and saw the shadows. Out of fear they came to me and hoped I would protect them. My master has always provided for us, been kind to us, and now my children say he is no longer below. They have gone to his other houses and have not found him there either. It's only right that I figure out what has happened. Don't you agree?"

Kalliope sighed. She almost felt bad for the spider. "Yeah. I agree. I'll help you and all, but I think we have to agree on something before we get into anything stranger than this."

"And what is that?"

"Whatever we come across, I'll try to not have anything squish you and you promise not to eat me even when we're at the end of this. Deal?"

Ginger pressed the points of her legs into Kalliope's sides. It made her stop and instantly regret what she had said. With one snap, those fangs could wrap around her neck and cut it clean off. "A spider's word is as strong as their web. Any spider that goes against a promise deserves their fate."

"Sorry, but then again, you have to realize I don't talk to spiders all the time."

"I'm sure, in your world, you step on them and keep going on with your day. I should feed you to my children for the deaths of my relatives, but I will not. I'll see this through until the end, and if you help me, then I will not eat you."

"Thanks. And honestly, I can't tell you if I step on spiders or just ignore them. I don't remember anything about my life. I was nameless until a woman in black told me what my name was. She said that if I went with her, she could restore my memory."

"Why didn't you go with her?"

Kalliope paused at the end of a corridor. It was a dead end, so she could only go left or right. Each way ahead led her into darkness. "She hurt someone. I couldn't go with her and leave Corrine to die. I had to try and help her, but then her husband came back and misunderstood the situation. He and the rest of the village attacked me. They called me a witch, hit me with stones, and I fell into their town well. There was a hole at the bottom of it that I crawled through, and I ended up in your sanctuary."

The spider snorted in disgust. "Humans. They're brutal animals. I don't understand them."

"You ain't kidding. I don't understand them either. I'm not sure what to tell you, just that I really want to get back to my normal life, whatever that is." She ran her finger over the ring and felt a jolt of warmth go over her. For a moment, she was very sad and wanted to cry. She didn't understand what was going on, but she wanted to know who was searching for her, and if it meant dealing with a talking three-foot spider, then so be it. "Which way do we go? There's no light up ahead, and I can't see in the dark. You know this place better than me. Where would your master be?"

"If you go left, it eventually leads out. If you go to the right, you will end up in the bowels of the temple. That's where you will find my master and the entrance to the Underworld. It's there that you must go."

"Great. Do you know how I'm going to see?"

"There is fire down this corridor and to the right. It has always been kept burning. It is a light so the spirits of the dead kings can find their way to my master."

"Who is your master anyway? I assume it's the dog-headed figure I keep seeing."

"Anubis is. The Lord of the Dead should be revered."

"Great. Good to know. Until we get to the fire, can you warn me if anything comes out of the dark that might want to harm me?"

"I will keep you safe. Don't worry."

"Thanks."

Taking a deep breath, she went right. After a few steps, she was immersed in darkness. The spider tightened her grip on her back. Kalliope stepped into the hallway and listened. Silence. Nothing was in there with her. At least not that she could see. *I can do this.* Touching the wall with her fingers, she eased down the long passage. The air thickened and there was an oily smell to it. Not sure what else to do, she kept on going forward.

Chapter Six

Kalliope followed the direction of the scent, not sure where it was leading her. She did sense the passageway was long and narrow. Her instincts also said that there was something else in the temple with her. It wasn't a person, but a power, a feeling of being watched, even in the darkness. She saw a pinprick of light at the other end of a corridor. Fire burned in a small bowl with no wick or any oil that she could see. The air wasn't moving in the corridor. It was in a small alcove, so the light was contained. No shadows were allowed to escape the small niche. However, there was a torch off to the side of it, and brightly painted symbols around the bowl.

She grabbed the torch, excited to see where the hell she was going, and went to put it to the fire.

"I wouldn't do that if I were you," Ginger warned.

She sighed. All she needed was the spider on her back telling her what else to do. She'd had it with the eight-legged insect using her as a pack animal. "Really? Why is that? I thought you wanted me to find your master. I need the light to be able to see. Not all of us are able to see in the dark." Her stomach growled, and she was getting tired. The air was stale and dry. It was murder on her skin. Her lips were chapped, and she needed water. What remained of the rash she got from the camel hair was flaring up again from all her walking. All she really wanted was something to eat, drink, and to get some rest, but being with the oversized arachnid, she doubted that was going to happen any time soon.

"Don't get snippy with me, missy."

Kalliope took a deep breath and got her emotions under control. "I'm sorry. I'm tired, hungry, and I want to get my memory back. I didn't mean to snap at you. I'm about at my limits."

The spider crawled down from her back and then crept along the wall so they were face to face. Seeing her reflection a hundred times over in the spider's eyes was a little unnerving. Nevertheless, she saw the dirt smeared on her face. Her hair had come out of its binding. She pulled the mini sword out and let her tresses tumble down to her waist. It felt better. Not wanting to lose the sword, she wove it through the fabric of her dress at her waist.

"I understand, but we have to press on. I have to find Anubis. Once we do that, I can tell you how to get out of here."

Shock washed over Kalliope. The spider had known all along a way for her to escape the underground labyrinth and wasn't offering her any help. "I should take the fire and use it to get rid of you."

"You won't do that. You promised to assist me, and I don't think you're the type of human to go back on your word. From what you've told me, you tried to help that other woman who was attacked. Not many would do that. Do you want to know why you shouldn't take the fire from the bowl?"

"Let me guess. I'll be cursed for a thousand lifetimes and my soul will be eaten by demons. My flesh will be torn from my body by ravenous scarabs, or mummies will come out of the floor and take me down to the Underworld with them."

Ginger crossed her two front legs. "Are you sure you've never been to Egypt before?"

Kalliope chuckled. "I'm sure. So, what's the big deal?"

"There is a warning on the wall from the ancient priests. It basically says, 'If the sacred fire is removed, then the guardians of the underworld will come to reclaim it.' So, if you take this, you will have to suffer the consequences."

"I don't really have a choice, do I? Without it, I'm stuck down here in the dark with a talking spider that only now reveals that she can read ancient Egyptian writing. Or I can stumble about in the dark until I die of starvation and still not find whatever happened to your master. Or I can take it and deal with whatever happens. Look, I don't know who I am or who's waiting for me if I get out of here. I don't know how I can understand you or how I ended up in this Godforsaken place. I did give you my word, and I won't go back on it even though you seriously creep me out. No offense."

Ginger's fangs clapped together again. "None taken. I don't normally end up talking to pasty-faced humans who are stubborn as hell and won't listen."

Kalliope burst into giggles. Her lids were heavy, and the dancing fire was making her even sleepier. There was no other choice. She hefted the torch up again. "I get that we both have our secrets, but at least help me out here. If you can read the sign that says take a left turn here for the exit, please let me know. I don't speak Egyptian or read it. You know the way out of here, so I'm at your mercy. You also may know what might be around the corner. So if I get into any trouble, you have to help me out because, like you said, I have to carry you through this tomb. So at least cooperate with me."

"Fine. Shall we go?"

Kalliope didn't like her response. It wasn't a promise like the one not to eat her. She wasn't going to argue with her. Once she touched the tip of the torch to the fire, the flame jumped from the bowl to the torch. Holding up the torch high, she could see down the passageway. The hallway where she had come from was lined on both sides with the reposed and lifeless forms of hundreds of mummies. Holding her breath, she waited for something to happen since she had taken the sacred flame. After a couple of quiet seconds, nothing occurred.

"Well, nothing so far. Which way do we go?"

"Please keep the torch away from me," Ginger responded.

Kalliope held it away from her. Seeing all of the corpses gave her the creeps. Goosebumps rose over her flesh. She ignored the feeling of dread creeping over her. "Sorry."

"Go right and then the channel branches off about three hundred feet ahead. You will take a sharp left and then go down over three hundred steps. This will bring you into the entrance to my master's lair. When I was a tiny spider, I'd run these halls. I don't see any of my children's webs down here. Whoever has barred me from this place will pay."

Great, a vengeful three-foot spider. "Okay, well then, here we go. Do you still need me to carry you? Or can you go forward on your own?"

The spider tried to move along the wall, but wasn't able to advance. "Nope. Still need you to carry me." She jumped down to the floor and then crawled back up Kalliope's legs.

She tried to shiver, but before the spider had settled, the sand underneath her began to shift. She was pitched forward and ended up face to face with a mummy. The mummy's eyes weren't closed. They were wide open and staring at her. Its wizened mouth pulled away from its teeth and issued an ear-splitting shriek. She regained her footing and backed away. Her eyes widened. The leathery corpse turned its head with a loud crack of bone and stared at her. Kalliope backed up. When she did, fingers closed around her shoulder. Bony ones. With a quick jerk, she pulled away and heard another snap. The fingers on her shoulder tightened. She glanced behind her and saw that part of a hand was still attached to her.

"Get it off me!"

Ginger moved and then the hand was on the floor. The mummy that shrieked was answered by another mummy and so on, down the line. Kalliope couldn't cover her ears to block out the noise and had to endure the screams. She watched in horror when more of the stiffs came to life. *This can't be happening. This is something out of some bad horror movie that I've never seen. Or I might have seen and I can't remember what it was.*

"I don't think you should remain here," Ginger suggested.

"You think!" She took off down the corridor. "Can't you shoot some webs at them or something to stop them? If you can talk then you must be able to do some pretty amazing things. Come on, Ging, help a girl out."

A hand popped out through the sand and wrapped around Kalliope's ankle. She stumbled. The torch went flying but didn't burn out. The spider stayed on her back. Her spiny feet dug into Kalliope's skin and pierced her flesh. She tried not to think about it while the sticky wetness slid down her sides. She yanked her foot from the grasp of the hand. When she did, a sharp pain ran up her leg. She didn't know if her ankle was broken or just sprained, but either way, walking would be challenging.

The spider hopped up on the wall and jumped from side to side, all the while spinning a large web to block off the advancing living dead. Relief flooded through Kalliope. She dragged herself forward until the torch was in reach. Her fingers wrapped around the handle when a loud groan sounded behind her. More mummies were coming toward them from the other direction. The opening to a doorway lay a few feet away. *That must be the passage that Ginger said we had to go down.*

"Ginger, can you go to the other side?" Kalliope gestured toward the marching mummies.

The spider hopped over her and began weaving another web. Once the torch was back in her hand, Kalliope heard a loud moan behind her. She dared a glance back and on the floor, eye level with her, was another mummy. Only this one had red eyes and a modicum of intelligence in them whereas the others were acting out of whatever ancient curse she had triggered. Something about those eyes jarred a deep memory. It wasn't clear, but she knew they weren't friendly.

"Oh crap!" she muttered.

The corpse turned its thin lips into a smile. It rose from its sandy grave and began to amble toward her. This thing was not going to let her get away. She crawled toward the opening using the torch for leverage to help pull her along. Ginger was twisting another web, but the mummies were getting through the first one she'd woven.

"What do you want?" Kalliope asked.

The mummy pointed directly at her.

"Yeah, I don't think that's going to happen. Let me guess; you don't want me going any further. Right?"

"Right," the mummy repeated. The hollowness to its voice was eerie.

She glanced at its eyes one more time and saw they were wider, more alive. The veins in them were red and more pronounced than they had been a moment before. Her head began to spin. The stiff's jaw dropped, and her mouth yawned open. Part of her wanted to give in to the corpse. Something began to reach inside of her and pull on her insides. Her arm moved of its own accord and started to hand over the torch. The walking dead reached for it and had sharp claws. *I can't do this. I need to keep the torch, but I can't help myself. It's doing something to me. I can feel it pulling my will.*

Then a sharp pain awoke her from her trance. She jumped back before the mummy touched her. She glanced at her arm and saw a smear of red on her flesh and Ginger next to her. The wound was fang-shaped. "You bit me!"

"Deal with it." Ginger shot a strand of web from her underbelly and it landed directly on the mummy's face. "That's not an ordinary mummy. That's Ammut. You mustn't look directly into her eyes or let her touch you. If you do that, your soul will be sucked into a vacuum."

"Great. Thanks for the warning. Who is Ammut?" Kalliope asked, pulling herself up. She clenched the torch and hobbled her way along the passageway. With each step, bolts of pain shot up her leg. It was all she could do to walk.

"No time. Get through the doorway. She won't be able to follow you there." Ginger scrambled along the wall next to her.

Kalliope glanced back and saw the mummy standing up. It looked pissed. Strands of linen swayed while it walked. Its eyes were clear of the webbing, but it was having a tough time seeing. Whoever was inside the corpse was not friendly. It obviously didn't want her to find out what was going on with Anubis. Pulling herself along the wall that was vacant of mummies, another hand grazed her other ankle. She jumped out of the way this time. Ginger shot another web at the rising mummy. The strangled cries of the other walking dead filled the hallway. They were beginning to get through the web Ginger had spun. Ammut was almost on her.

Kalliope dashed through the hallway and then stopped. She had forgotten the spider told her to take a sharp left. Good thing she stopped because before her was a dark pit. If she hadn't stopped, she would have fallen to her death.

Backing away a step, she saw the stair passageway to her left. Ammut's fingers raked her arm, but when Kalliope pulled that closer to her body, she realized that the creature wasn't able to pass through the doorway. Ginger was right. The mummy pounded on the invisible barrier and then screamed. It narrowed its eyes and pointed at her.

"I will get you." It formed the words slowly, and each was filled with menace. Kalliope trembled, but her ankle was killing her. The corpse disintegrated into the very sand it had risen from until there was nothing left except the skull. The moans of the dead reverberated throughout the hall, calling for the reclamation of the lost flame, but they couldn't pass through the door either. There wasn't any way for her to go back. She had to go down.

"Ready?"

"I guess. Not like I can go back. Why couldn't Ammut come through the door along with the others?" she asked Ginger.

"The glyph above it. It is a ward."

She glanced at the top of the door and saw an ankh through a large eye above the door. She would have to remember that for later use. "Hmm. Works for me. So, now we go down the stairs and descend into the awaiting darkness."

Chapter Seven

Kalliope leaned against the wall and tried to ignore her throbbing ankle. It was badly sprained and starting to swell, but she had to keep going. Her fear was building due to what she had already been through with the mummies and whoever Ammut was. Ginger waited for her on the steps. She tottered, trying to get away from the wall, but she needed it for support and wasn't sure if she could carry the spider's weight much longer. Holding onto the torch, leaning against the wall, and trying not to fall down the stairs were problematic enough.

"We must go onward," Ginger pressed her.

"Yeah. I know. But first we have to clear some things up."

"What things?"

"Who and what was that thing back there? And you bit me!"

Ginger clapped her fangs together, laughing. "I had to bite you to break her spell. Ammut is a demoness. She is ruled over by Ma'at, the weigher of souls. Ammut shouldn't have been able to manifest in that way, but it appears that she is out to get you. Ma'at keeps a strict leash on her and only sends her out to collect souls."

Kalliope shook her head, not really sure what to make of the news except that she had a demoness on her butt for some unknown reason. "Thanks for breaking her hold over me, but next time try to do it some other way before chomping on me. I don't know if I can carry you down these stairs the way my ankle is. Can you try and walk beside me or behind me maybe?"

"I'm okay now. I was only blocked from that particular passage. Thank you for bringing me this far. Now we must go on." Ginger began to scuttle down the stairs and headed into the darkness.

"Oh, Ging, wait up. I can't move that fast." Kalliope called into the blackness where the spider had gone. After a moment, the spider came back up.

"Sit down. I might be able to help you."

"You're a spider. Unless you have magickal healing powers, I doubt it."

"Humans. Please, sit down before I decide to web you up and leave you here."

Kalliope sighed, slid down the wall, and sat on the step. She glanced back and saw the mummies were crowded at the doorway still unable to get through. Their yowls were muffled from whatever obstacle was keeping them out. It still sent chills down her spine. She hoped she'd never see that congregation again unless it was in a horror movie. The spider poked at her ankle with one of its legs. Each time it did, she drew in a painful breath. Glancing at her ankle in the light, she saw it was swollen and turning colors. *Maybe something's broken.*

Ginger stood up on four of her legs and then began to spin a web, which she balanced between her four front legs. Her legs moved faster and faster until something shone in the middle of it. It appeared to be a long bandage made from webbing.

"Lift your foot, please."

The spider wrapped the makeshift bandage around her ankle and tied it neatly in a bow. It was tight, but it wasn't cutting off the circulation. She clutched the torch and tried to place her weight on her foot. When she did, it seemed that it wasn't hurting as much. The web wasn't any weight at all, and a tingling began to envelope where the web-bandage was. "Thanks. How did you know how to do that?"

The arachnid gazed at her. The torches reflected in each one of them, making her appear demonic. "Spiders can weave anything we set our mind to. And you're forgetting that I used to feed on humans. My web dulls pain. If wrapped it all around you, it would put you in a state of suspended animation until I was ready to eat you. Of course, once I injected the venom into your bloodstream, you'd be paralyzed."

Kalliope shivered. She really didn't want the spider on her bad side. "Great to know. Thanks. I'll try not to piss you off."

Ginger didn't answer, but turned and began heading down the steps. Kalliope followed, clutching the wall for support and the torch in her other hand. After a few steps, she realized they were on a spiral staircase. Down about ten steps, the wall had fallen away, and the only thing holding up the staircase was a long column that was inscribed with pictures of all different kinds of things. The largest thing she could make out was the painting of the black jackal-headed god. She stuck close to the pillar, not really trusting her ankle because it twanged a little here and there. The spider stayed beside her, and once she was fifty steps down, she looked back up and saw that the temple above them had disappeared. She couldn't see the bottom of the cavern she was in. For all she knew, she had stepped into a different world. With everything that was happening to her, Kalliope wondered if she was involved in some magickal debacle that was playing out between the Egyptian gods.

Another fifty steps down, Kalliope stopped. The stone pillar continued downward with the stairs wrapping around it. The torchlight only extended so far, but the single light didn't do anything to illuminate the abyss of silence she was in. The air was still. The atmosphere was tepid. The only sound that echoed around them was the tapping of Ginger's legs on the stone steps. The silence was eerie. The flames glinted off her ring. A pang of longing went through her. She tried not to dwell on it. Her heart was heavier for some unknown reason the more she thought about who had given her the ring. Something inside of her insisted that she had done something to exact this course of fate upon herself. *I don't know what I said or did, but I'm sorry. I miss you, whoever you are.* For a split second, a feeling of love overtook her, eclipsing her loneliness. Tears came to her eyes, and even though it was nice to think that she had made some unconscious connection to the one who gave her the ring, it only made her lonelier.

"Are you okay?"

"Not really, Ging. I need to get out of here and figure out who I am." She wiped her eyes and trekked onward. Kalliope wondered if she would end up in China, or maybe at Lucifer's front door. She had lost count of how many steps she'd gone down, but it was more than the three hundred that her arachnid companion had originally told her it was.

When she hoped they were getting near the bottom, she heard a noise. It was a massive train-like roar rushing toward then. She stopped and tried shining the torch into the darkness to see what was making the racket, but only the continuing blackness met them. The pillar that held up the stairs no longer had any paintings or carvings on it. It was only pale tan stone that was smooth and cool to the touch.

"Can you tell me where we're going? We've been walking down these stairs forever, and we must be hundreds of feet below the surface. You said you knew this temple. So any hint you can give me would be great. I'm seriously thinking that something supernatural is going on here. Maybe that's why I can understand and talk to you. Demons and walking mummies don't happen all the time."

The spider jumped onto the pillar so they were eye-to-eye. "We're heading down into the Egyptian Underworld. No human that I know of has ever been this far underground. The priests were only allowed to go a hundred steps down. That's why the paintings ceased. I used to take these steps ages ago with Anubis, but then he asked me to go above and guard the entrance to his temple. I never liked humans much, but you're turning out to be okay."

"Well, that's good to know. Hopefully, I won't end up dead and a permanent resident." Kalliope thought about what she said, that no human had ever been down this far. *Does that mean I'm only human? Or does that mean I'm something else? Obviously something odd is going on, but I have nothing to base it on because I have no freakin' memory of it. Maybe I'm a fallen god and this is my punishment. Gee, what did I do to end up in the middle of the desert? Did I desire to be human? Was I ever human? I don't know. All of this is off the wall, and I'm going into the Underworld. I hope they have some great drinks because I'm going to need one after all of this is over.*

They continued down more steps. She stifled a yawn and noticed the air was growing steadily cooler and moist. The roar was louder the further they descended. They didn't talk. A breeze began to blow the flame around. Gusts of wind began to come up around them. It was hard for her to hang onto the pillar. She inched her way down, but the spider didn't have any trouble. Kalliope stood with her back against the column and felt wetness on her cheek. She dabbed it away and saw it was water. She ran her tongue over her chafed lips and tasted the droplets. They tasted fresh. It was then she realized that the roar she was hearing and the wind was being caused by a massive waterfall.

She walked to the edge of the stairs and stretched the torch as far as it would go. When she did that, she was able to see part of a waterfall glistening in the fringes of the torch light. At that moment, she saw movement. She wasn't sure what it was, but from the way it moved, there was more than one, and it was big.

"You ever know of anything else that inhabits this place?" Kalliope caught up to the spider a few steps down.

"There are certain guardians, but I don't think they'd bother you."

She saw more movement out of the corner of her eye. Then a loud shriek erupted next to her ear. Kalliope glanced up at the pillar. Large fanged teeth were inches from the top of her head, filling the mouth of a creature she wasn't sure how to describe. It had bat wings, but a round head with slits for a nose. Neon green eyes glared at her while strings of black saliva stretched from its maw.

She screamed and bolted down the steps. Her ankle was wobbly even with the webbing. The thing jumped off the column and glided down at her. It pulled its wings into its body and increased its speed. Kalliope jumped out of the way and barely kept herself from pitching over the edge of the stairs. Another creature came at her head. She ducked just in time to see Ginger shoot a web at another thing coming straight at her.

"What are these things?"

"I don't know. They weren't here the last time I was down here, but that was over a thousand years ago."

Kalliope waved the torch at them, trying to fend off the creatures, but they were coming too fast. One caught its wing on fire and went up as if it were made of dried wood. The other shrieked and bombarded Kalliope. She lost her balance and dropped the torch. She reached for it, but wasn't able to catch it before it tumbled into the oblivion below. One of her nails cracked, but she kept her balance. The things tried to attack her, but Ginger seemed to be fending them off. Another creature hit her from the side. This time, she pitched over the side of the steps. She grabbed the air, but her other hand caught the edge of the stairs. She glanced down and saw the light was bobbing about, but it still hadn't gone out. The wetness from the waterfall settled in her hair. She tried to lift herself up, but she wasn't strong enough.

All at once, she felt a sticky substance on her hand. "Grab onto it!" Ginger yelled.

Kalliope tried to do that, but the web wasn't strong enough to hold up her weight. She held onto it, but the blood from her torn nail made her grip slippery. Instead of holding onto the sticky web, she slipped from the skein.

The air whooshed around her. The sound of the waterfall masked her scream. She didn't know how far she fell, but the light from the still lit torch was getting closer. The air rocketed around her faster. She had no way of stopping. She shut her eyes tight and prayed, but her thoughts turned toward the one who had given her the ring. *"I don't remember who you are, but I'm sorry. I can't call out to you, but however I ended up here or wherever I'll go after I'm dead, I'll always love you. I know that. Forgive me for whatever I've done that might have hurt you for.* Deep grief filled her being. She truly was sorry for anything she'd ever done, even though she didn't know if she'd hurt anyone. However, she was sorrier that she would never get to gaze upon that man that she loved. That was all she wanted. She prayed that in her death, she could see him and be able to say goodbye. Whatever god protected her, she hoped she would be granted that one thing.

The cacophony of the waterfall grew louder. She pressed her eyes shut. The water splashed against her face. Even though she was sad, she also felt a deep sense of peace fill her. She was okay with dying because she had tried to help out a friend. Not that she ever would have considered a three-foot spider a friend before, but why not?

At that moment, her feet hit the water first. Breaking the surface of the water knocked the wind out of her. It also made every bone in her body feel broken. Once the darkness of the water encompassed her, she sank. The current wasn't very strong even though there was a great waterfall frothing up the water.

Kalliope let herself drift, unable to move much since everything hurt. It was peaceful being tossed about. Her lungs burned for air, but she didn't mind it. It was an odd feeling. She was detached from her body, and it seemed like she was floating. Before she could enjoy the sensation, something grabbed a hold of her and began pulling her up. After a few seconds, she breached the surface of the water. She breathed and took in life-giving air. Her whole body throbbed. She opened her eyes and was able to focus on someone above her. It was a man.

"Kalliope, are you okay?"

She sat up slowly and wiped the water from her eyes. Her torch was set in the sand a few feet away from her, and Ginger was hopping down the last few steps. The man before her was drop-dead gorgeous with curves in all the right places. There was a faint sweet scent around him. She licked her lips. His dark hair fell across his forehead like pieces of shaved chocolate. She reached out to touch him, but found that her hand passed through him. He seemed to be a ghost.

"What the hell? That has to stop happening," he said.

Kalliope wasn't sure what to make of him. "What has to stop happening?"

"I don't know what it is, but ever since I woke up here, my power has been flickering in and out. It's like I'm disconnected from my body. Sometimes I'm solid, and other times I'm not. This is very strange."

She wasn't sure what he was rambling about, but he reached out and took her hand. This time, it didn't pass through hers. The inside of his palm was soft and silky the way whipped cream was on the top of a cheesecake. The image of a cherry-covered cheesecake came to mind and then she shook it from her thoughts. Her stomach growled. *It has to be because of the lack of food.*

"What are you doing here anyway?"

She gazed into his intense hazelnut brown eyes. "I'm sorry, but do we know one another?"

He seemed puzzled. "Kalliope, it's David. You know, the hunky, smooth cheesecake god that you lust after all the time."

She glanced at her ring and back at him, but her gut said that he wasn't the one who gave it to her. She shook her head. "I'm sorry, but I don't know who you are. And really, are cheesecake gods real? That seems a little absurd."

He stood up and dusted himself off. After a moment, he snapped his fingers and his very shape changed. She gasped because before her was no longer the deviously striking man, but a large, plain round cheesecake. All his appendages and his facial features appeared as if they were off a Mr. Potato head doll. She backed away. This whole scenario was already a bad nightmare. Now it was just getting worse.

"Good God, what the hell are you?" she cried.

The cheesecake's red plastic lips turned into a frown. His plastic, round, black eyes squinted. The more she gawked, the more she found him comical. There was no way this being before her was a god. Of course, she was saying that three-foot talking spiders didn't exist either, but they did. He walked toward her with his oversized white hands outstretched to her. "I won't hurt you. Whatever they did to you, you have to know I would never hurt you. You mean too much to me for that to happen."

He reached out and touched her chin. When he did, his appearance changed. Fleshly fingers touched her skin instead of the fake limbs she had just seen. His gaze bored into hers. Whatever magick he had pressed upon her evaporated. She smelled vanilla and peppermint. She licked her lips. He leaned in to kiss her, but stumbled right through her. Kalliope gasped at the sudden cold chill that followed.

"Argh. This is so annoying. Let's try this again." His brow furrowed, and she couldn't see through him any longer. He gave her a cocky grin and kissed her lightly. At first, she didn't mind the kiss. It was soft and nice. It made her remember that somewhere out there, people did exist, and she wasn't stuck wherever she was stuck. David deepened the kiss. His power washed over her full force. She got all hot and bothered and began to return the kiss, but halfway through, it didn't feel right.

Placing a hand on his chest, she reluctantly separated from him, already missing the warmth of his body. "I'm sorry, but this...whatever it was, although it was really nice, you and I aren't together in that way. I may not know you, but I do know that. Whoever I'm with, I really wish I could remember him. Do you know him?"

David touched her cheek. Her knees shook when he did, but she was not going to let her body dictate whose arms she was going to fall into. She was all about finding the person who gave her the ring. "They never should have done this to you."

"Who did what to me? Please, if you know something, will you tell me? I'm tired, hungry, and pretty banged up, not to mention soaking wet." It was then she realized how she appeared. Hair a mess, transparent dress clinging to all of her body parts, a swollen ankle that was killing her, not to mention everything else since she hit the water pretty hard. She hated to sound desperate, but that was how she felt. She'd come this far and still had no answers to what she was doing besides descending into the supposed Egyptian Underworld. *Maybe he does. Maybe he can help me.*

He opened his mouth and a translucent film shot out and covered his lips. He immediately began pulling the web from his mouth. She glanced over and saw Ginger a few feet away. Her fangs were opening and closing almost as if she were out of breath. Considering their journey and all, she probably was because she hadn't been all that active in who knew how long.

"Do you want me to wrap him up for you and put him on ice?" Ginger asked.

David wiped the web from his lips. "What the hell was that for?"

The spider jumped between the two of them. "I saw what you were trying to do to Kalliope. You were enticing her with your power. I bet you were the one who barred me from finding my master! I'll wrap you up in my web so quick you won't have time to call upon your magick. Once I get you into my web, it'll neutralize you."

He put up his hands and backed up. "Whoa! Whoa! I'm not sure what's going on here, but I wasn't trying to make Kalliope do anything she didn't want to do. I respect her enough to know better. She's engaged to a good friend of mine. I can't help it if she's a beautiful woman and looks the way she does. It happens. Chemistry and all. And I did not block you from getting down here. I don't even know where here is. The last thing I know was that I was at Lugh's bachelor party. Then we were attacked by some crocodile thing and I blacked out. You're the first thing I've seen besides these flying whatever they are."

She was stunned when he said a name. *Lugh!* It resonated deep within her soul. Her ring flashed red, and then the spark died inside of it. It seemed her soul was dying too. The glimmer flickered in her memory, but she wasn't able to dig any deeper with it. That alone caused her grief. *What have I done?*

"I don't believe you. I've seen your kind before. Made up gods who fizzle out when people stop believing in them. You have power and then you go *poof*. I know you were the one—"

"Enough! Both of you. Just get over it and deal with it. Who cares if he'll go *poof* tomorrow or if you can wrap him up in ten seconds flat and tie him up in a neat bow? I'm tired of this. I just want to be left alone for awhile." Kalliope shook her head, picked up the torch that had washed up onto the land, and headed into the darkness. The others started to follow her, but she put her hand up and shook her head. She needed to think straight. She needed answers. Her body hurt. She was hungry, she could barely walk because her ankle throbbed, but more than anything, she was heartbroken.

Chapter Eight

As Kalliope walked down a long hall, she noticed a basin running along both edges of the corridor. She glanced inside and saw glistening liquid in it. On a whim, she touched the torch to the fluid. The flame jumped from the torch and immediately ran along the oil. All at once, the hallway was illuminated. She was rewarded with seeing the corridor lined with reclining black stone jackals. Their golden eyes moved with her while she walked. Something in her told her that if she posed a threat to whoever or whatever was down at the end of the hall, they would come to life. She sighed and ran her hands over one of the stone creatures, wishing she were made of stone also so she wouldn't have to keep feeling the despair that nestled in her breast.

The walls were painted with reliefs showing the water with people floating down the river. At the end of the river was a large sun with Anubis welcoming them. Next to him was a woman with wings presiding over all of them. The more she studied the river and the woman, it seemed that they were moving. Kalliope sniffed and found she was crying. She hobbled down the hall and wiped her tears away. Her body began to shiver, but the fire was warming things up. She half expected more mummies to come out of the stones and run her off. She turned with the hall and went a few more feet until she came to a set of large wooden doors. The symbol for the sun was used for the knobs. Fear rose in her while she listened for movement. She heard nothing behind them.

Her fingers touched the intricately carved doors inlaid with gold in the hieroglyphics, and the door swung inward, opening before her. The basins of fire ran through the wall and into the interior of the room. This was the hub of the temple. Slipping between the doors, she gasped at the beauty of the place. Golden idols of all different kinds of figures were set around the room. The ceiling was vast, and the whole place smelled of sandalwood. Sarcophagi stood in the corners of the room with four canopic jars placed next to them. An empty throne sat in the middle of the pillared hall. Once she entered, she heard the patter of feet and low growls. Fear crept inside her heart. From the shadows, five large, snarling jackals appeared. She kept going forward. The beasts snapped at her, but she didn't balk.

When she came to the throne, she saw a tray of food laid out along with a pitcher and a glass. She wasn't sure if she was supposed to eat it, and even though her stomach was gurgling and making a ruckus, she wasn't going to touch it. Instead, she walked around the throne. Behind it there was a vast amount of gold trinkets along with clothes and a bed. The bed appeared more inviting than anything else. Even though it was also tempting, instinct told her not to lie upon it. Peering around the hall, something about the columns struck a chord. Even the fire seemed familiar, but she couldn't grab onto the memory. Another pang of longing shot through her.

She hobbled over to a stone pillar, aware the creatures were circling her, and slid to the floor. She laid her head back against the column and stared at the ring. Nothing came to mind. She put her face in her hands and began to let the dam of emotions break. Everything that had happened to her she really hadn't had a chance to process. She had been on the go since she'd been picked up and thrown in the well. She had to keep going, or she might've been killed.

Now her mind and body were broken, and it felt like her spirit was also.

"Why? If this is some sort of test, haven't I passed it? No one should be put through this," she whispered. "Lugh, whoever you are, please just let me remember something. How you look or what you sound like. Something." She sobbed until her chest hurt. A whine sounded next to her. Then a wet nose nudged her palm. She glanced up. One of the jackals was staring at her with amber eyes. It bumped her again and wanted attention. She patted its head for a moment, feeling the short hair under her palm. Kalliope chuckled when it lay on its back and then rolled over, showing her its belly.

After a moment more of scratching, she heard clapping. At the applause, she gazed up to a woman in dark robes with her face covered. Kalliope recognized her from the village earlier. However, she wasn't sure which one she was until she saw her gold-tipped nails.

She rose and faced the woman. The jackal's hackles rose, and it snapped at the newcomer. Kalliope thought it was odd that they had all of a sudden thought she was a friend and not a foe. Maybe she had some magickal touch when it came to animals. "What are you doing here?"

"You don't know who I am yet, do you?" the woman asked.

"How would I know who you are when I don't recollect anything except waking up in the desert? You told me I would suffer the consequences if I didn't come with you. Well, here I am. Now tell me who you are and what the hell is going on!"

"You love Lugh even though you can't remember who or what you are. I think that's impressive, but would you love him if he were a gnarled old man, or a fierce, deformed monster?"

Kalliope shook her head. *Who would ask such questions?* "It doesn't matter if he was a cockroach. I'd love him no matter what. Even though my memory is gone, our bond isn't. I know I love him. He's my other half, and I'm his. There's nothing else to be said."

The woman removed her veil and shook out her long, dark hair that fell in waves to her waist. Her ebony skin glistened in the fire light. She snapped her fingers, and her black robes changed to a clingy white dress with a large gold ankh dangling between her breasts. Kalliope felt the majesty of her presence, but she wasn't put off by it. Again, it stirred something inside of her.

"I had to be sure that was the reason you were marrying Lugh and not because of the power you'd inherited. Or the thought that one day you might end up a goddess. I needed to know he's going to be taken care of. You're still human at the core, and humans are petty. They want power. They love seeing others get hurt so they can have their way. I didn't want you to end up using Lugh and then throwing him away after you'd married him a couple of centuries down the line."

"Why would I get tired of the man that I want to be with? Why would you even think that unless you're in love with him, too?"

The woman laughed. "In love with him! Well, that might be putting it mildly. Lugh and I had our flings. I think he's been with every goddess in the astral realms, but when you caught his attention, I thought little of it. Nas was chasing after him, and you were nothing more than a blip on my radar. Then his infatuation didn't wane. It grew to the point where he proposed to you and gave you a piece of his heart. Hell, you even befriended his ex-lover. Then you made me wonder. I wasn't able to do anything about it while you were dealing with the Greek problem. They are always so disorganized. When I got back from my vacation, I saw the perfect opportunity. I watched you for a little while, and you reminded me of when my husband was alive. We were so good together, Osiris and I. And then he got himself killed. He never should have died. You shouldn't have made it this far."

Things began to fall into place for Kalliope. "So you were the one who took away my memory and dumped me in the middle of the desert, because you wanted me out of the way. You wanted Lugh all to yourself. All of this sounds typical even though I still can't remember why. You make me go through hell to see if I was worthy of loving the man you haven't gotten over? Now that I've survived your tests, what are you going to do to me?"

Kalliope's blood pounded in her ears. She clenched her fists together. *This is all bullshit. She's wanted me out of the way since the beginning. Now that I survived, what is she going to do? I really need to break this enchantment and find out who I am.* The jackals growled again and bared their teeth at the woman before her.

"I wasn't the one who took away your memory, Kalliope. That wasn't my idea. I'll take credit for the ingenious idea of wanting you out of the way. Part of this test was also someone else's design. Only I set the rules that if you died, there wasn't any harm done. You have to blame—"

She raised her hand. "I don't want to hear any more. Sic her, boys. Goddess, or whatever you are, I'm sure you won't feel it. I'll deal with the other culprit behind this when I figure out a way out of here."

The jackals advanced on the woman. She began to laugh. "You won't hurt me."

They bared their teeth and got ready to spring. Once the goddess realized that the animals weren't going to stop, a look of panic crossed her face. "Nice poochies. You don't want to hurt Mama Isis now. Come on. Be good boys."

Kalliope watched the beasts circle, and noticed David and Ginger at the end of the throne room. David was flickering in and out of focus. She headed toward them while the goddess screamed behind her. She almost glanced back to call off the dogs, but she wasn't in any mood. She wanted to go back to wherever she had come from, take a nice long bath, eat, and make love to a man she didn't remember all because a stupid bitch still had the hots for him and wouldn't admit it.

"Can either one of you get me out of here?"

"What about Isis?" Ginger asked.

Another scream erupted behind her. "I don't care. David, can you make yourself whole long enough to take me to Lugh so I can get my memory back, please?" She crossed her arms over her chest.

He opened his mouth and then nodded. "I can sure try. It's troublesome for me to stay solid. There's nothing to keep me here. What about spider woman?"

"I haven't found Anubis yet, and Kalliope said that she'd help me."

"I didn't say I was going to stop helping you. Obviously, he's not here, and if Isis survives, I don't think you want to be around when the dogs are done with her."

"Aren't you afraid of what she'll do to you?" Ginger asked.

"Not really. Shall we go?" She slipped her arm through David's and found him to be solid. *Thank goodness. I really don't want to stay here anymore.* Ginger crawled up her back and settled there for the ride back.

"Away we go."

* * * *

After a moment of disorientation, Kalliope found herself standing in a room full of women. At the very end of the room was a table where a shrine had been built. On top of it was a man that looked like David lying peacefully. Flowers were placed all around him, along with spatulas, mixers, candles, and other sweet treats. Candles burned behind him on a shelf that gave the room a sweet smell of vanilla, cinnamon, and strawberry. Kalliope licked her lips. Her stomach growled.

David slipped away from her and dashed toward the memorial. "What the hell is my body doing there?"

Everything stopped around them. All of the guests stared at them with stunned expressions. They began to talk in rapid succession so much it hurt her ears. There were two babies in the corner being entertained by a flying bullfrog the size of a Thanksgiving turkey, and a short woman with long, dark hair came out of a kitchen carrying a tray. At that moment, she dropped the tray.

"David! Kalliope! You're alive."

Kalliope smiled wryly, not sure who everyone was or why there was a shrine in the center of the room. David began poking at his body, but his hand kept moving through it. When Ginger jumped off her back, screams erupted around the room. Some of the women leapt onto the couch to get out of her way. Kalliope took in the different women and felt some kinship with all of them, but wasn't able to sort through it all.

"Of course I'm alive. It appears I'm difficult to kill, even though that was the plan."

"David, we all thought you were gone. You can't imagine the hysterics I've had to deal with in Avalon. Where did you find her?" the dark-haired woman asked.

"She found me, Morgaine. I'm not quite sure what happened. The last thing I know was that this crocodile chick came to Lugh's bachelor party. The next thing I remember clearly is seeing Kalliope plunge into the water. I jumped in and pulled her out."

"Ahh, I hate to interrupt, but where's Lugh?" Kalliope asked Morgaine.

"Kalli, are you okay? Surely you know that Lugh has been scouring the underworlds and astral realms for you. Now that you're back, all you have to do is just call out to him."

"How do I do that?"

Morgaine gave her a funny look. "Seriously? What the hell happened to you, and where did you dig up the spider? I haven't seen one that big since Merlin conjured one to try and scare me off. That's a funny story."

"I'm sorry, but who are you again?"

Morgaine chuckled. "Very funny."

Another woman with blonde hair and glittery skin stepped forward and touched Kalliope's cheek. She stared deep into her eyes and a sad expression came over her. "Do you know who I am, sweetie?"

"I'm sorry, but no. Who are you?"

"Ahh, can someone tell me how to get back into my body, please?" David asked.

No one was paying attention to him.

"I'm going to kill him. I'm Flidais. We're good friends. So are the other women here. No one will hurt you. We've all be so worried about you. You've been gone for a week. Lugh's been tearing up Heaven searching for you. All Hail doesn't appreciate it very much."

"What wrong with her?" another woman asked. She had large breasts and deep, piercing eyes. Something about her made Kalliope tremble, almost if there were some unresolved feelings there.

"Hello. Body please," David said with his arms crossed over his chest.

Kalliope and Flidais both glanced at David. "We'll deal with you later. You're not going to die. So hush." Flidais focused back on Kalliope.

"Her memory's been erased, and her power has been bound, Nas. Not to mention she's hurt and probably starving," Flidais told the other woman.

Kalliope wanted to answer when there was a loud boom in the room. A light brighter than the sun appeared for a fraction of a second and then disappeared. In its spot was a man with blond hair and stunning green eyes. He was dressed in black leather pants, had a sleeveless emerald vest on, showing off blue serpent tattoos, and a gold torque around his neck. Once she saw him, her soul knew it was Lugh.

"Where is she?" He pushed through the crowd until he was standing before her. He was so regal and stern she scarcely believed this was Lugh. Seeing him was overwhelming. The love inside of her exploded and brought new tears to her eyes. Part of her wanted to bow down and kiss his feet in worship. She understood that she was in the company of gods.

"Lugh, there's something you have to know before—" Flidais began.

But he scooped her into his arms and crushed her to him. Once he did, Kalliope knew she was home. Nothing else mattered but being in his arms. She inhaled his heady scent. It made her dizzy, smelling of wet leaves and sun ripened wheat. Her entire being hurt, but it didn't matter because she was back with him. His lips sought hers, and she returned his kiss. At first, it was soft, and then insistent. Stars exploded inside her mind from the sheer power that hummed through her, his power. It didn't frighten her; it only made her crave more. He ended the kiss too soon. He brushed the hair from her face and peered into her eyes.

"Kalli, do you know who I am?"

"You're, Lugh. The man I'm going to marry. The man I love." Kalliope wanted to tell him more, but wasn't able to. She could see that wasn't the answer that he truly wanted.

"Do you remember anything about how we first met?"

"Lugh, buddy. Sorry to interrupt you, but can you help me out?" David chimed in again.

Lugh gave David a look of annoyance. He waved his arm. When he did, David disappeared. Kalliope looked over at his body on the shrine. After a few moments, the cheesecake god began to stir. Then he swung his legs over the table and stood up. When he did, he gave her a sly smile. He stretched and flexed his fingers. She tore her gaze from him and glanced back at Lugh. She searched her memory, hoping the spell had broken now that she was home, but it hadn't.

"No. I'm sorry. I want to, but—"

He placed a finger on her lips. "That's okay. Close your eyes for me, love."

She did what he asked. His hands touched her temples. Her hair grew hot, and she began to sweat from the power he poured into her. It withdrew in a moment, and she opened her eyes. She still didn't remember anything. Lugh held her in his arms protectively and faced Flidais.

"Why would he do this?"

"I don't know. You have to ask him."

"Kal, I want you to stay here." He began to move away, but she grabbed onto his arms.

"No. Please. I can't—" She couldn't tell him now that she had found him, she didn't want to let him go again. Kalliope might lose him again. She couldn't deal with that.

"Shhh…okay. You won't ever lose me. Hold on." He hugged her tight. Being with him was all she needed to stay sane. After everything that had happened to her, she needed him to protect her. The world whooshed by and, with a *pop*, they were standing in the middle of Times Square. Lugh let go of Kalliope so she could take in her surroundings.

Everything around her had stopped. A gaggle of people were crossing the street. Cars were trying to weave through them. The signs were frozen. The dog next to the large palm tree had stopped mid-pee. She smiled at that.

"Dagda, stop pretending to be a palm tree waving at everyone. It's not funny anymore. We need to talk now!"

Lugh got brighter the longer he talked. At the end, she had to shield her eyes. The atmosphere contracted. When the light died away, another handsome man with red leaves in his beard and dark blond hair stood where the palm tree was. The new man eyed her and gave her a devilish smile. She didn't return it, but shrunk away from him.

"Kalliope, you look worse for wear. Have you been mud wrestling? Did you and Isis get into it? I can see you two now. Your glistening bodies tangled together under—"

Lugh stepped between them. "I said enough! Why did you bind her powers and wipe out her memory? Why would you put her in such danger, especially with Isis? You know she's crazy. Why would you make me tear apart the astral realms hunting for Kalliope? To hurt her is to hurt me."

Dagda's face fell. His expression darkened, and his skin got paler. "It's none of your business, Lugh. What happens between Kalliope and me is our business. Isn't that right, dumpling?"

She stepped further behind Lugh. A deep sense of dread filled her as she stared at the other god. "Please, don't let him touch me."

"See what you did. The woman I love was never this timid or afraid of you. Restore her memory and unbind her powers. Whatever scheme you have going on or reason you think you had to do this, it's over. Fix this now."

"And what will you do about it? You're not as powerful as me. With one swipe I could strike you down where you stand the way I did Cromm. You know the pecking order in the realm. The head of the pantheon always has the most power."

"So this is about power? I get it. You think that because Kalliope was going to marry me, I was suddenly going to want to take over your throne. Haven't I always been loyal to you? She's done everything you ever asked her to do. She kept her promise to you when you sent her to Mt. Olympus. She saved the gods from Hephaestus's plot. She brought Flidais back to you. Or doesn't that matter anymore?"

Dagda pointed his finger at Kalliope. "We had to be sure that she was in it for love and not for power. She had to be tested. Isis made me help her. I owed her a debt. By Universal Law, I had to repay her. Isis made the rules of the test. I didn't want to do this to Kalli. I love her like my own. And I had to know if she was true. We had to be sure if the bonds between you would survive. Isis didn't say anything about wanting her killed. I didn't know she was jealous of your relationship. She hasn't been all that steady since Osiris was killed. I tried to intervene where I could. I put the hole in the well and the tunnel so you would find the temple."

Lugh flicked his hand and a sword appeared in it. He pointed the tip under Dagda's chin. Kalliope wasn't sure what to do. A line of crimson stretched down the god's tan skin. "Isis could never let me go. You of all should've known, debt or no debt, that it was wrong. You've been my father. How could you!" He pushed the tip deeper into Dagda's flesh.

Dagda reached out with his hand. "Excalibur. Come to me!"

Kalliope felt the wiggling near her waist and saw the small sword moving from the cloth. Instantly, it hovered and grew longer. It flew to the other god's hand, and when he had it, he touched Lugh's blade. Blue sparks appeared on the metal. Lugh parried and avoided the arc from Dagda's blade. Lugh backpedaled, hit one of the frozen pedestrians in the middle of the street, and sent him flying.

Kalliope screamed. He got up and reached for his fallen sword.

"Stop this, please!"

Lugh glanced at her and smiled. "Don't worry, love. He won't hurt me." He dodged another strike and then struck one of his own. A thin line of blood appeared on Dagda's chest. The god didn't seem to be fazed by it. Dagda swung again, but Lugh jumped back. She cringed when Lugh hit a lamppost and it fell to the ground. The glass shattered and scattered on the pavement.

She leapt out of the way and went behind Dagda.

"Lugh, I admire your attempt to fight me, but don't piss me off more. I did what I had to do. You understand how Universal Law works. Kalliope was bound to it when she accepted my offer to go to Mt. Olympus and help out Zeus."

"Screw Universal Law. Sometimes you can ignore it, especially when it comes to the woman I love. She's practically one of us. That means you have to get her permission to do anything to her." Lugh kicked Dagda and caught him in the knee. The god fell to the ground, but didn't lose his grip on the sword. Lugh stood over him with the blade at his neck.

"Sometimes Universal Law can't be ignored, and at the core, she's human, so what does it matter?"

"It matters to me. It should matter to you, too. What happens one day when we have children? Would you say the same for them?"

Children? She hadn't gotten that far yet. Heck, that was a surprise, but she knew better than to bring it up. "Guys, enough. Let's just forget all this happened. Dagda, give me back my memory, and we'll call it even." Kalliope begged both of them to stop. Lugh turned to say something and Dagda got up and stepped toward them, but tripped, careening right into Lugh. The sword stabbed Lugh's side.

A shocked expression came across his face and then pain. Immediately, time started again.

"No!" Kalliope sank down with him and caught Lugh in her arms. She didn't care about the blood staining her hands, but held him close to her. Dagda knelt down on the other side of him.

"I didn't mean it. I swear!" Dagda touched her arm.

"I don't care. You took everything away from me. I've never done anything to you. He loved you—" She broke down into tears.

"Forgive me." Dagda brushed the side of her face. At that moment, memories and images raced through her mind. A gush of warmth came over her. She only held her lover closer because she remembered everything now.

"Get away from me, Dagda."

Lugh drew in ragged breaths. His face was gray. She felt him slipping away. Now that she'd just gotten her world back, it couldn't be taken away from her again. She opened his vest and black lines were shooting outward from the wound. She never imagined that Dagda and Lugh would fight. There had never been any animosity between them. She pressed her hands to the wound and tried to will it to heal.

"No use, love. You can't save me," Lugh wheezed.

Wetness slipped down her cheeks. She hugged him. With all her might, she willed herself away from the craziness and cramped streets of New York to a much quieter place. When she opened her eyes, she found she was in the same grove where he had proposed to her. The very first one in which he had revealed himself to her. His fingers entwined with hers and squeezed hard. He was trying to hold on, but any wound from Excalibur was fatal.

"You can't leave me."

"I'd never leave you. Every time the sun rises, that will be me. I'll always watch over you. I love you."

She pressed her lips to his. The more he faded away, the more a part of her died also. Coldness replaced where his warmth used to be. His essence was slipping away even faster. The wound wasn't healing. The light was dying in his eyes.

Kalliope kissed his forehead and held him to her. Her tears ran freely down her face and wet his cheeks. She wiped them off and felt how cold his skin was.

"I love you," she whispered.

"I know." He took her hand and kissed the back of it. "Before I die, I give you my birthright."

"No. Save your strength. Please. Someone has to be able to do something." Kalliope sensed another presence. She gazed up and saw Flidais lingering on the side of the grove. There were tears on her lashes, and the sadness she saw was the same that she felt.

"There's nothing you can do. Please accept what I'm offering you before it's lost. Please!"

"What is it? I already have part of you inside of me. You gave me your heart. That's all I need."

There was a hand on her shoulder. "He wants you to take his godhood. That way no one will be able to claim his power. With it, you'll become a god."

"No. No. Lugh, I can't. I don't want it."

"Please. Promise." His voice was fading. He was already cold to the touch.

She nodded and sniffled. "Okay."

"Kiss me, love." Lugh gasped.

She glanced at Flidais, who nodded. Kalliope pressed her lips again to Lugh's mouth. Pain seared her flesh and ran down her spine. It felt like she was expanding all at once. She couldn't control it. It was ten times the experience that she felt when she made love to Lugh. She clutched him to her until the feeling passed. She felt lightheaded and wasn't sure what was going on, but Lugh was cold in her arms. He was limp beneath her. She opened her eyes and lowered him into her lap. His vacant eyes stared at her. Seeing him lifeless drove a wail from her throat.

"No! You can't leave me! No." She hugged him to her and couldn't stop the wracking tremors that began to overtake her body.

"Kalliope, he's gone. Come on, sweetie. You have to let him rest. There's nothing else we can do for him. Let me take you back to Dagda so we can sort this all out and find out who did this to him."

She stared at Flidais. The woman had been a good friend to her, but she would never have anything to do with Dagda again. "No. *He* was the one who did this to Lugh! He was the one who did this to *me*! I don't care how much you love him. He's dead to me."

The goddess was flabbergasted. "He would never. Never! He loved Lugh. He was his flesh and blood."

"He did. I saw it with my own eyes. You can't tell me that he didn't. I saw him. Excalibur wounded him and now he's dead. Gone."

Flidais touched her again, but she shrugged out from her embrace and clung to Lugh.

"Leave me alone! I just want to be alone with him!" All at once, the world shifted. There was a bright light and then a blast of wind. She glanced around and saw she was on the shore of a vast still lake. Mist blanketed the pond. The scent of apples permeated the air. The fog parted, and she saw a pale man dressed in black robes walking over the water to her. She clutched Lugh, unwilling to let him go for anything, not even for whatever creature approached. The man knelt beside her. He had dark hair, long, sharp nails, and deep, sympathetic dark eyes.

"Who are you?"

"I'm here to take him to his final rest."

"You can't have him. Please, I can't let him go." She felt her power rise up and try to push him away. It was so strong that she wasn't sure how to control it. It burned her insides. The little hairs on her arms ignited in flame.

The stranger placed his hand on her shoulder. The power cooled inside of her, and the fire died on her arms. It felt like she was plunged into an ice bath. She glanced into his dark eyes. Inside them she saw a burst of silver and then there were stars deep inside. This wasn't an ordinary being.

"I know you don't want to let him go, but you have to. Even gods have to go to their final rest. You kept your word, and he knows that you love him, but you have to let him be at peace." The being's calming voice rang through her mind. It didn't help ease her sadness; it only made her handle it better.

"What are you?"

He smiled and showed her long canine teeth. His nails left light scratches on her wrist. "What do your instincts say, Kalliope?"

She tried to sort through all the feelings and memories that swirled inside her. The longer he held her hand, the more her thoughts made sense. She was able to concentrate on him. "You're an angel. You're the Angel of Death."

He nodded and released her hand. "I am. My name is Azrael. I was called by your pain, and I sensed the loss of your beloved. Normally, gods aren't escorted to the other side, but Lugh was born human. He retained a soul even after all these years. He loved you. Still loves you. You carry a piece of him on you. Keep that bit handy. It will bring you comfort."

He went to pick up Lugh's body, but Kalliope wasn't going to let him go. Azrael glanced at her and then nodded. Peace infused her body, and she knew that she had to give Lugh up. She nodded too, and kissed her departed lover on the forehead. "Goodbye." She wiped a tear away and released him, feeling the loss inside of her soul.

"Don't worry. I'll take care of him." Azrael gave her another smile and wrapped his body into his cloak. When he turned and began to walk away, Kalliope reached out and touched his dark cloak. He stopped and faced her. She felt there was more to him than just an angel. After everything she had seen, she was surprised that there really were angels. When he turned, Lugh was no longer in his arms. She wanted to ask him where he went, but decided against it.

"Why you? You're a high angel. Why would you come and take him? Why not another angel?"

"Because over the years, Lugh and I have become friends. I know many beings that span many planes and many worlds. You'll see that I am friends with all of them. I understand what it means to lose the one that you love. I've had that experience, but you'll be surprised what the universe holds. Don't let sadness consume you. It'll only eat you alive. Don't push your friends away, no matter how much it hurts. If you need me, I'll be there for you. All you have to do is call out." He took her hand and brought it to his lips. A cold zing ran through her and put out the fire in her core. When he backed away, he grew fainter, and the mist surrounded him until the fog swallowed him.

Kalliope watched until he was gone and she was alone on the vacant beach. The reeds whispered a sorrowful song in the light breeze. Tears streamed down her face freely, adding to the rain that was now falling on the island. In the distance, she heard the unearthly lamenting of fairies. She wiped her eyes and saw beings that she had never perceived before. They weren't like the fairies in the oak tree. They were human and small, gathered at the edge of the wood. All were dressed in white shifts with blue tattoos on their faces and arms.

A woman walked toward her. She had a wreath of flowers in her hands. Kalliope saw a small blue crescent between her eyebrows. Her sorrowful expression grew clearer the closer she got. In her outstretched hands was a wreath of white and purple flowers she offered to Kalliope. She knelt down. The wreath settled on her head.

"What's this for?" Kalliope asked.

"It's our gift to you. You have lost your love and we were going to give these to you at your wedding. Now you have entered our hearts. You have seen the dark angel, have been touched by sorrow, and you have also been touched by the cosmos. You're recognized by Excalibur and have found your own path to the island. This is the true isle of Avalon."

Kalliope was surprised to hear that. She'd been to Avalon, and there were people there. Morgaine Le Fey was the priestess on the island. "What about the place where Morgaine is? I thought that was Avalon."

The fairy shook her head. "No. The priestess has created her own Avalon. It is a reflection of the true island that has not gone into the mists. Morgaine's place is in between the between. Think of it as a long skip from your realm. From her realm, it is only a small step to that of the gods. This is the true island. No human life has been here in centuries. Arthur's grave is beyond the hill over there. The sword has chosen you for its champion. We would have acknowledged you earlier, but we are out of time with even the astral realms. It's hard to explain the shift of time, but since you are now a god, you can travel to whatever realm you wish. However, that is irrelevant. We share your pain. Lugh was well liked among the fey. Please know that you are welcome to come here whenever you wish. You have my condolences."

"Thank you."

The fairy queen nodded and then began to back away. Their songs didn't stop, but only reflected what she was feeling. The music soothed her soul only for a little while, and all she could do was focus on the lapping water and wonder if she would ever feel happy again. Or would she remain forever frozen?

Chapter Nine

Kalliope didn't care how long she sat and stared into the unmoving gray water. The mist wrapped around her over the land, blanketing the landscape in its cold embrace. The wind trailed over her flesh, but it didn't affect her. She wasn't cold. Hunger and thirst didn't plague her. It was a strange experience, but she didn't think on it the way she used to dwell on the changes that magick did to her. What did it matter now? She was a goddess because she had taken Lugh's godhood, but that wasn't anything she ever wanted. All she craved was to have him back in her arms. The warmth of his power kept her from freezing, but it didn't do anything to bring him back. If she thought about it, she could feel the world and the universe around her, but again, what was the point? Nothing in the world would ever be the same again. Nothing in any world was going to be the same again.

The grayness of this Avalon, the one out of time, was the place where she truly belonged. The fairies had withdrawn back to the woods, but they kept watch. Once Lugh had given her his power, all her wounds had healed. She could see herself in the motionless lake's reflection. To say she was beautiful was an understatement. Every flaw she had was gone. His power had remade her into a perfect being. She'd never have to worry about shaving her legs again or ever getting a wrinkle. Her skin had the same glittery quality to it that the other goddesses had. That didn't matter. She could be sparkly as a star, but without her sun to share the sky with, her heart was dead.

The wind blew her hair in her face. She pushed it back only to notice it was black and white, reflecting her mood. Her dress was the color of night, and her skin was ashen. She wondered if she screamed if the world would shake or volcanoes would erupt. Maybe she'd set off torrential floods with all her tears.

Kalliope was above her coven sisters and didn't even feel them connected to her anymore. Lugh's magick seemed to have burned away the links they shared, or she was keeping them out. Either way, she couldn't share her grief with anyone. It would be easier for her to turn to stone or bury herself beneath the sands of Egypt, where she'd found herself only days before, and wait for thousands of years until some archeologist unburied her and wondered why she wasn't mummified.

Sleep tugged on her, but she wasn't tired. All her emotions swirled inside her heart. She glanced at the ring on her finger. The stone hadn't lost any of its luster. It was warm and still a part of Lugh. It was the only thing she would be able to touch of him forever.

"Why couldn't it have been me?" she screamed. "Why did you have to take him?"

The wind wailed around her. She saw women in black and green dresses flying over the lake. Their shrieks were a reflection of her soul. Black and filled with so much anger that she needed to take it out on someone. She peered into the vast sky and didn't see the sun. All Hail was there somewhere, but it wasn't him that she was pissed at. There was only one god that she had to deal with. The keening women drew closer until one hovered above the water. Her eyes were completely black. Her skin was pale and wrinkled. Her teeth were pointed and yellowed with green and black spaces between them.

"What is your bidding, my mistress?"

Kalliope wasn't sure what the being was. "Who are you? Why have you come here?"

The woman cocked her head to the side, and all she heard was the sickening crack of breaking bones. "We are the bean sidhe, the banshee. You summoned us with your cries. What would you have us do?" The woman bowed before her.

Kalliope stood up. "What can you do?"

The leader snickered. "Anything you wish. Our cries will kill a human. We cannot kill a god, but we can hurt them. Do you have something in mind? Perhaps the one who brought this heartache upon you?"

She smiled, liking the train of thought that the banshee had. "Yes. Do you know Dagda?"

"We are aware of the Greenman. He's always been kind to us, but we know what he's done to his grandson. For that, he must pay. There'll be other gods around him. They will sense your presence. We can cause a distraction for you. Our screams will not affect you, but the others, we can make sure they don't get in your way. You can bring him back to this place and then take out your anger."

"Yes." The creature's words made her feel somewhat better. Taking out her regret on the one who had done this to her would relieve some of her pain. It wouldn't solve the problem, but Dagda had to pay for what he'd done. She didn't care what the others would think.

The banshee bowed and Kalliope saw an evil gleam in her dark eye. She straightened her dress and ran her hand through her hair again. The power inside of her glowed, but it made her cold instead of warm. That was exactly how she wanted to feel. The banshees gathered around her in a protective circle. They would be her entourage. Once the others understood and figured out what was going on, Dagda would be dead.

She saw herself inside the great oak tree that was his refuge and seat of power. Within a moment, she had transported herself and the banshees with her. A collective hush settled over the crowd. Kalliope saw a gathering of gods and goddesses she hadn't seen since Cromm had claimed her for his concubine. Dagda sat on his throne. Flidais was in the corner stirring her cauldron. The beaver was in another corner chewing on some wood and fashioning a set of bowling pins. The fairies suddenly all dropped from the lily chandelier above her. The one promise she had made to the fairy queen came back to her. She was supposed to get her a date with Dustbunny, the goblin. However, that didn't matter now. The warm atmosphere grew cold. Kalliope saw her breath when she exhaled. The moss and grass beneath her feet turned brown and then black.

Dagda sat up in his throne and didn't take his eyes from her. Excalibur was sheathed around his waist. It wasn't time for her to take the sword back yet, but she did sense the weapon. Its link was stronger with her now.

"Kalliope, we've been expecting you." Dagda rose and stepped toward her. She didn't move.

The frigidness radiating from her was becoming more intense. Ice formed on the barren ground. The blue oak apples she'd originally eaten to gain her magickal powers turned brown. The whole tree shook. Dagda's appearance didn't change.

"Dagda, you and I have some unfinished business."

He walked toward her with open arms. "Come to me. You're my daughter now. What happened was an unfortunate accident that I regret, but it has brought you closer to me." His smile faltered when she didn't move.

The power inside of her flowed outward and touched everything that was in the tree, including the other goddesses. She heard their teeth chattering, and they were now focusing their power on her to try and get her to stop what she was doing. The branches of the great tree began to tremble. Icicles formed inside the chamber. She glanced at the great wooden throne with the stag headpiece where Dagda sat. It was now covered in a sheet of ice. She raised her hand and formed a fireball in it. With one lob, it hit the throne and shattered it into a million splinters. Dagda staggered back and covered his heart. His skin began to grow paler and his hair white.

"Kalliope, stop this!" Nas screamed behind her.

She turned and saw the goddess was gaunt and her hair black. Kalliope reached out her hand and found the center of Nas's power. With a thought, she pulled it into herself. The woman collapsed on the floor and didn't move. She began to draw on the other gods' powers and freeze more of the tree. While she did Dagda aged.

Then she was struck with a harsh sting across her back. She glanced behind her to see Flidais holding a ball of fire in her palm. "Kalliope, get a hold of yourself."

She ignored her and glanced at the banshees. "Girls, have your fun."

"Do we have your permission to draw on the fallen gods' powers?" their leader said.

"Go for it. Leave Flidais be, though. You won't touch her. Understood."

"Of course." The banshees opened their mouths and wailed. They fanned out until they had all of the others covered. She didn't care what happened to the other gods. It was only her and Dagda now.

"Do you think this will accomplish anything?" he asked.

"It will accomplish what I want." She grabbed his arm and willed them both back to Avalon. When they got there, she was thrown to her knees. Her head spun. It seemed she was using a lot of her power and wasn't able to keep siphoning from the other gods now that she was gone.

"Having trouble?" Dagda asked. He seemed younger, but his handsome façade had fallen away, leaving a man of fifty behind with sagging skin and dark circles under his eyes.

Kalliope stood upright and didn't acknowledge she was losing some of her power. She didn't care. She didn't know what would happen when she was out of juice, but if she burned up the sun using it, then at least the man who killed her beloved would be dead. She reached out her hand. "Excalibur, come."

The sword disappeared from Dagda's side and was in her hand. It felt good to have the familiar weapon. In her head, their link flared to life. It didn't want her to do this. It hadn't wanted to strike Lugh, and it felt bad.

"I don't blame you. Don't worry about it. There's only one man who took Lugh away from me. You were only the instrument. Will you help me now?" she asked the sword.

The blade glowed blue and then black, filling with her sorrow. She began to draw upon the sword's power, and her will overtook it. The bond between them grew, and she became the weapon. One touch from her and she could kill a god. She opened her eyes and focused on Dagda.

"It won't do your bidding. It won't let you kill me."

Kalliope chuckled. "You have no idea what it will do. It chose me as its champion and now its will is mine. You stole Lugh from me! You stole my memory because you had to prove that I wasn't out to marry him and become a goddess and get power hungry."

Dagda gazed at her. She sensed him trying to gather his power, but he was cut off from it. This was her place. She ruled here. This desolate land was her kingdom, and he wasn't going anywhere.

"Kalli, I never knew what Isis was going to do to you. I did her a favor. I never realized that she was still pining over Lugh. It was an accident. I never meant to kill him. I couldn't stop before it was too late. Do you really think I wanted to see him dead? Or have you end up like this? You said that you never wanted to abuse your power. Now look what you're doing. You're taking his power and twisting it. What do you think he would say if he saw you? He wouldn't want you to end up this way."

Tears fell from her eyes, but she didn't lose her grip on the sword. A gust of wind whipped around her and lifted her up a few inches so she floated above the grass. "It doesn't matter now, does it? He's dead. He can never come back. You took him from me! You have to pay!"

Dagda stepped toward her with his arms outstretched and knelt. She brought the tip of the sword to his throat. One nick was all it would take. Once the essence of the blade was inside of him, it would kill him the way it had her lover. His dying image flashed inside her mind and fueled her rage. His vacant eyes. His pale flesh. Those luscious lips that would never kiss her again.

"Get up and fight me!"

"No, Kalli. I'll sacrifice myself. It won't bring back Lugh, but I hope it will ease some of your anguish. Then you can call off the banshees. They're using you. They want power. They felt your sadness and were drawn to it like moths. Kill me if you wish, but let the others live. Would you kill Nas and Flidais, who are your friends? Would you wish to rule over all the Celtic gods or even All Hail? Your grief will drive you into insanity. Now take my head." He took the tip of the blade and brought it to the back of his neck.

Kalliope raised her arm. Before she could strike, she saw the man before her with frog legs hopping around and making her laugh. She saw the one who was doing cartwheels repeatedly because he was addicted to caffeine. She saw him smiting Cromm and saving her from an eternity of servitude to the death god that her grandparents' coven had once promised her to. She shook her head and thought of Lugh. Maybe if she died too, he would be there for her one day, but now that she was a god, she didn't know when that day would be. In her mind, she saw Lugh kneeling before her. He and Dagda were so much alike, both sun gods, both regal and valiant. Lugh had adored him even though he drove him crazy once in awhile. He wouldn't have wanted Dagda to die over something so trivial.

She brought down the blade, but before it hit his flesh, she dropped it and sank to her knees. She crumpled to the ground and cried all over again. Thunder rattled the sky along with the land. Rain pelted all around her. She felt arms embracing her and stroking her hair.

"I'm sorry. I'm sorry."

"Shh…it's okay. It's okay. We can deal with this. First, you have to drive the banshees back. Do you wish that?"

She nodded. "Yes."

A loud wail erupted around her. She felt the coldness of their presence. "Why have you revoked your permission?"

She stared at them. "You don't need a reason. Give back the power you've stolen and go back to the dark realm you came from." She gritted her teeth and willed it to be so. The leader screamed again. Once she did, the whole troupe exploded in a dark shower of ravens. She felt the power leave them and rush back through Dagda.

"Now you have to give back the power you stole."

"I don't know how to do that."

"May I kiss you?"

She pulled away and wasn't sure if she could trust him, but she knew that what she'd done to the other gods wasn't fair. Her sorrow had drained away and left her only with a large pit of remorse where her soul had been. Kalliope nodded and waited for him to kiss her and bind her powers the way he had done before.

"I'll never do anything to hurt you again. I swear it." He raised her hand to his lips and kissed the center of her palm. The warmth inside of her began to be drawn down her arm and he was sucking it back into himself. After a few moments, she felt deflated. Dagda returned to his normal self. He helped her up and then pulled Excalibur from the ground. He handed the sword to her. "I think this belongs with you."

She shook her head. "I don't deserve it. I wanted to kill you, and I made the sword want that. I can't be trusted with it." She ran her hand over the pommel and felt it spark back to life. Excalibur shared her sympathy. *Give me a little while, okay? I don't want to be hacking away at other gods anytime soon.*

The sword glowed purple, and she felt its acceptance and reluctance. It wanted to be with her and help ease her suffering, but she didn't trust herself with the weapon right now. Dagda hugged her close. Her tears didn't seem to stop. The thunder rumbled again. Lightning lit the sky and made the lake choppy. The wind whipped around her, trying to tear away pieces of her very self.

"This place isn't good for you. It's only for the dead. I don't think any human has been to the true Avalon in ages. Not even Morgaine comes here. The way is closed to her."

"Where exactly are we?"

Dagda sighed. "Avalon has become more of a gateway between here and other dimensions that we gods traverse. I bet you reached out and your grief brought you here. Now you have made yourself one with the land. You have to break your hold with this place, or you'll end up slowly rotting away inside, and the woman that you knew, that Lugh loved, will be no more. The power will grow cold and not burn hot. You would become nothing more than the banshees that you summoned today. That's what a banshee is. A woman so heartbroken that her rage and anguish has transformed her into one of the twisted creatures you saw today. We deal with them because we have to, but I don't want you to go down that path. Will you come back with me?"

Kalliope gazed around. At the treeline, she saw the fairy queen. The petite woman smiled and nodded. She wiped her eyes and turned her attention back to Dagda. "Yeah. I don't want to stay here. It reminds me too much of him. And I'm ready to go and face whatever punishment I have to for attacking you and the others. I know it was wrong."

The god hugged her closer. "Don't worry about it. It's forgotten. Come." The world moved around her, and they were back in her apartment. The place didn't feel right. She sensed Lugh all around her. His dog was sleeping on the couch and lifted his head. He whined when he saw her. She shook her head and willed herself somewhere else. When she opened her eyes, she was in a space she'd never been before. It was a flat dais that looked out onto mountains. The sun beat down and warmed her, reflecting on the white marble all around her. This place reminded her of Mt. Olympus. Everything was carved with the emblem for the sun.

"What is this place?" Kalliope asked.

Dagda was right behind her. "This is the place where all the sun gods are recorded. It's like a giant sundial. Each column has an etching marking each of us." He led her to one of the pillars. "This one was Lugh."

Kalliope ran her hand over the gold circle that was a simple disk with another circle carved inside of it. Runes were engraved into the stone that she could read now. She moved to the next pillar. It was blank. A gold light appeared, and then fire smoldered from the stone. When she could see again, she saw her name. Below that was a circle with a cross inside of it. She ran her fingers over it. "What does this mean?"

"It means that you've been recognized as a sun goddess, but also one that is more. You've been able to touch all elements because you were a witch. Lugh gave you a powerful gift."

"I don't want it. I'd give it back just to have him back." She rested her head against the pillar and willed herself not to cry. She had to use his gift wisely and not take advantage of the power again.

"I know. Come on. The reason you were brought here was because the heavens have found you worthy and now you're recognized as one of us. Seems All Hail thinks that you can handle the power. He's the last one that has say over all of us. Evidently, he feels you're okay with it."

"Can I ever talk to him? All Hail, I mean?"

Dagda stroked his beard. "We barely ever get to see him. Only if there are emergencies. Even if you were to get an audience with him, he would deny resurrecting Lugh. It just isn't done."

Kalliope's heart dropped. She had hoped, but now her hope was gone. She didn't want to argue with the head honcho, but she did want to see him and ask him why. If All Hail was the leader of the universe then why had he done that to her? Then again, that was a question she had asked growing up when her parents died. She ran her hands over her arms and suppressed a shiver. "I get that. Can we go now?"

Dagda touched her shoulder one more time. They were whooshed away. When they reappeared, they were back inside the oak tree. Everyone had cleared out except Flidais and Nas. Dagda sat down on his throne, which was whole again. The self-playing harp strummed "Eternal Flame" by the Bangles. She wasn't sure how to handle it.

"I'm sorry about before. I didn't mean to hurt you." She kept staring at the grass and watched it coming back to life under her feet. Where her tears fell, white flowers sprung up from the ground.

Flidais put her arms around her and hugged her. "It's okay. We all lose our temper."

Nas joined in the hug. "We're okay, Kalliope. Don't worry. No one blames you for what happened. We're all feeling his loss. I understand how you feel."

Kalliope wiped her eyes and smiled at the two women. Beyond them, she saw someone that she recognized. It was her Aunt Constance. She unwound herself from the goddesses and ran into her aunt's arms. The ghost was realer than she'd ever been before. She kissed her on the top of the head. Immediately, she felt protected. She had come home, and this woman could chase away any demons she had.

"Hi, sweetie. I'm so sorry."

"Thanks. I don't know what I'm going to do without him."

"You'll be okay. Your heart will heal in time. Come, dear. I have a surprise for you."

Kalliope eyed her. "Please no apple pie. I can't stomach it right now."

Constance laughed. "No. Come on." She took Kalliope's hand and began to lead her away. Before they got to the recarving wall, the same goddess that she had ordered the jackals onto stood there with faint scratches on her and a torn dress. Her hair was a mess and sticking out all over the place.

"Where do you think you're going?" she seethed.

"She's coming with me," Constance said. They moved past her when Isis grabbed Kalliope's arm.

"I don't think so, old woman. You have no power here." Isis pushed Constance backward. "You, Kalliope, are going to pay for giving me to those jackals. When I get done with you, you won't be able to dig yourself out of the pyramid I put you in."

She went to take Kalliope when Constance stepped in front of her. "Isis, enough! Leave Kalliope be. She's suffered enough."

"What are you talking about?"

"Lugh is dead, Isis." Nas told her.

"Dead! That can't be."

Nas looped her arm through Isis's. "Come on."

Kalliope didn't say anything to Isis and didn't feel any sympathy for the goddess. She held onto Constance's hand. A feeling of peace washed over her. They walked through the wall and when they emerged, she found herself in a beautiful garden that she'd never seen before. Among the flowers were her parents.

"How?" she asked Constance.

"All Hail thought this would alleviate your pain. I'll come back when you're needed."

"Thanks." Kalliope turned and walked into the waiting arms of her mother.

Chapter Ten

Kalliope ran her fingers over a lily, feeling the silky softness of the petal. Its white trumpet blared with life. A bumblebee settled on her fingertip and sat there before waddling down into the center of the flower to gather pollen. Even here, in this place, the edges of Summerland, life went on. Her mother sat underneath a willow tree on a blanket. It was strange to have spent so much time with them and see her reflection; they were practically identical.

Being with her parents helped relieve some of her suffering, but it didn't take away the heartache. The more she was with her parents; the more she realized she would never be happy again. A piece of her soul had died. Life moved on around her, but her life had stopped. Now she was trapped in immortality without anyone to love. She envied her parents. They had died together and had one another. Even as ghosts, she could see they were soul mates, so when they reincarnated, they would come back together. She wouldn't have that opportunity with Lugh.

"Kalliope, come sit before you have to depart."

She gazed at her mother. The thought of leaving them wasn't something she wanted to fathom. This serene place gave her a reprieve from the heartache that weighed on her shoulders. Once she went back to the real world, she'd have to deal with her obligations. There were too many of them; she didn't want to count. Her head spun. She sat under the willow tree with her mother and threaded her fingers through the lush grass. The smell of the blades was sweet and mingled with the vast flowers. There were so many she didn't know the names for them. In the distance was a bright light that blinded her. That was the entrance to Summerland, into Heaven, where she wasn't able to go.

Her mother patted her hand. "Penny for your thoughts?"

She tried to smile, but wound up having her eyes tear up. Lately, she hadn't been crying, but grief stabbed her heart. "Just thinking about what I'll have to deal with when I go back. How I'm going to go on and all. I just wish—" She shook her head and wiped her eyes. Sometimes she wondered if there were any more tears inside of her.

Her mother hugged her. "Sometimes you wish what?"

Kalliope took a moment and regained her composure. With all the time she had mourned, she'd also had time to think about everything that had happened when she lost her memory. She understood now that her Egyptian adventure had been a test, but she had also said that she would help Anubis and Ginger. She had done her part with Ginger and reunited her with the death god. She had to get Ammut off his butt and hers too. She had no idea about Isis, but she really didn't care. They might have lost the men they loved, but she was not going to turn into that psycho.

"I want to do my own thing. I'm tired of getting involved in the turmoil of the other gods. They all come to me now. Not just the gods, but elves, goblins, whatever. I want to live the way a normal human would. Is that so bad? I wanted Lugh and me to be happy. Have children. Run the business and watch Teresa, Anna, Adele grow old together and enjoy their magick. I didn't want to be a goddess or some second coming of magick or whatever. I just wanted happiness. That was the only thing I truly craved when I summoned Lugh."

"Would you give it all up?"

Kalliope sighed. "I-I don't know. Not the magick or the friends I've made, just the crap that goes along with it.

Heck, I saved the world, and now I'm roped into something else."

"You've never been one to back out on your word. Would you go back and change the past? You have that power, even though it's risky."

She stared into the bright light of Summerland, feeling the peacefulness of the world beyond the doorway. If she could go back and change the past, she would make sure her grandparents' coven never promised her to the death god Cromm. If she did that, then she'd never have met Lugh. Her parents would still be alive. There were too many possibilities to think of. Time wasn't something she wanted to mess with. And she would never go back on her word, no matter how much of a pain in the ass it was. She would help the other deities and then she was done. She owed everyone that much. Maybe then she could go back and live her life selling candles and bath soaps. It would seem like a humdrum existence, but that was the one that she wanted now that she didn't have her sun god to share it with.

In her mind, her days were going to be forever cloudy with a chance of showers. The sun would never make an appearance to dry the water. Dagda's warning about her turning into a banshee danced through her mind. She knew that wasn't something she wanted.

"No. I won't go back in time. And I won't go back on my word. I think that was one of the reasons Dagda bound my power before all this happened. He wanted to see if he could trust me, or that was Isis's reasoning. I don't know. I just don't want to get involved in anything else unless it's to help my friends deal with ex boyfriends or how to raise their magickal children. Is it selfish to want happiness or normality?"

"It's not, Kalliope. But you have to remember that you're different now, so those parameters of what you want have changed because of what you've become. You know the phrase 'with great power comes great responsibility,' and I know you won't use your power for ill."

She nodded. "I only wish that power could bring him back. I'd give it all up for him."

Her mother picked up her hand and touched her ring. "Remember, you have a piece of his essence with you always. His power is inside of you. Those are all the things you need because they'll never leave you. Your love for him can make him live on."

She laughed half-heartedly. "If only that were true." She hugged her mother, sensing that Constance was waiting to bring her back. Her mother kissed her cheek and beamed. The pride in her eyes was overwhelming. Her father reappeared and gave her a small hug too.

"We'll always be watching over you," he said.

"I know."

She took Constance's hand and gazed behind her one more time into the light of Summerland. Her parents were glowing, but behind them she saw a figure standing on the boundary. One that she knew all too well. She reached out to it, but the light blinded her so she had to cover her eyes. When she took her hand down, she was back in her apartment with all of her friends gazing upon her, worried expressions on their faces. She hadn't thought about their reactions to losing Lugh, but now she saw the hurt they also felt. Constance didn't say anything, but patted her back and then faded out.

"You need to be with your friends, dear. When you need me, I'll make sure there's an apple pie waiting."

"Thanks." Kalliope didn't expect a response, but went into the waiting arms of her coven sisters. All her friends cried on her shoulders. She hugged them closer, glad to see they were okay. Now that she was back in the real world, she sensed that she had been gone for two weeks. It had

only felt like two days. Her friends must have been worried sick.

"God, you're so warm. Are you okay?" Theresa asked, pulling away from her.

"Yeah, and you smell like vanilla. You look amazing. Where the hell have you been? What the hell happened? Flidais and Nas told us what happened, but is it true? Are you really a goddess? What's that like? How did you get your hair to be so perfect?" Adele asked.

Anna nudged her cousin in the stomach. "Adele, shut up. We have to think about her well-being not about her hair care regimen."

Kalliope smiled at the two of them. They were complete opposites, but somewhere down the line, they had discovered they were related. She put up her hands. "I'm not okay, but I'm getting there. I don't know if I'll ever be the same again." She gazed at her apartment, feeling the energy of the circle she had in her living room. Making a quick assessment, she touched each of the quartz crystals that outlined the circle and willed them stronger. Once that happened, the energy of the circle intensified. Nothing was coming through this baby when she cast a circle.

The place was almost alien to her when she walked into the kitchen and felt the remnants of Lugh's magick. The spell he had placed on her cabinets and refrigerator remained. She closed her eyes and remembered the many times he had worn her pink apron, trying to flip pancakes for her. A smile played on her lips whenever she opened her freezer and it spit out chocolate chip ice cream instead of her favorite.

Lugh had appeared to her naked in the woods and then followed her home. She'd called nine-one-one on him, and they didn't believe her, so she'd eventually wrapped herself up in her shower curtain and went out to face him.

She wiped the tears away and glanced at her friends, knowing they were trying to cheer her up.

"It's good to see you. I'm sorry if I've been away. First, it was the amnesia thing with Isis, and then Lugh, and handling his death. I kinda lost it."

"Sweetie, you don't have to explain. We understand. We've all suffered loss in some form or another," Adele said.

"Yeah. Remember the time I was dating Waldo? We used to joke about where's Waldo and then he was actually two-timing me with some other chick. I really loved him. Broke my heart when I put that hex on him. Shame, too. I hear he still has problems with only the one testicle," Anna responded.

"And you have to remember how well you helped me out with Juan. The gorgeous hunk that thought he could swindle me out of my inheritance. You helped me make him believe I was a devil worshipper and that I would make his dick shrivel up if he ever did anything to me. Then you fed me cupcakes for a week while I sobbed and bawled my eyes out because I'd already had the wedding dress picked out." Adele giggled.

"Guys, that isn't the same thing. Kalliope lost her soul mate. Shut up about your botched relationships. You only had Waldo for like a month. Juan was your boy toy for six months that you paraded around in front of us." Theresa threw up her hands and opened the fridge to pull out a tray of chocolate truffles and a bottle of champagne. "Come on. You need a serious girl's night. I don't know if you can get drunk or not, but you need to."

Kalliope knew she wasn't getting out of this. "Fine. Fine, but tell me what's been going on. How are the twins? Are you still dating that demi-god? How's the shop? I'm so out of touch."

"Twins are fine. Shop's fine. I've been making these two man your shifts. Nas and Flidais have pitched in. You need more inventory, though. You're super low. Yes, I'm still seeing Barney. He's awesome in bed. All of us have been out on dates together." Theresa didn't meet Kalliope's eyes.

"Whoa. Whoa! You set these two clowns up with other gods? Come on. I already told you that—" Theresa shoved a truffle into her mouth. The smooth dark chocolate hit her and tasted heavenly. For some reason, it was better than any other chocolate she'd ever had. At once, she calmed down, and it didn't matter that her friends were dating gods.

"You want another one?" Adele asked.

Kalliope nodded and popped another truffle into her mouth. The second one tasted divine. She clenched her thighs together to keep the rush of pleasure inside of her contained. "What's in these things?"

"Something that you need so you can let loose." They all turned to see Morgaine standing in her bedroom doorway, holding Humphrey. Once her familiar saw her, his eyes widened and a huge grin spread on his face, showing her his pearly whites. The sorceress threw the frog, but he unfurled his white feathery wings and flapped toward her.

Once the amphibian settled into her lap, he snuggled against her breast and uttered a loud sigh of relief. She began stroking his smooth back and feathers. Each time she got to his feather tips, he quivered.

"Oh riibb-it."

"You're sick, you know that?"

He batted his eyelashes at her. "Oh, I know, toots, but it feels sooo good. Oh yeah, just like that. Stroke it like that one more time."

She obliged him and began rubbing the ridge of his wings until his back foot began thumping against her leg.

Kalliope winced and moved him onto the back of the couch. "It's good to see you too, Humph. Morgaine, I don't know what you put into the truffles, but oh God. I seriously need someone to ride out my tension on, but since Lugh's not here, I'll have to make do. How's David by the way? Did he get settled back into his body?" She closed her eyes and let the pleasure of the chocolate take her over. When she did, her magick surfaced. It began to burn off the effects, but it did leave her with a calm and peaceful feeling.

"David's fine. Don't worry about him. Cheesecake Factories are still operating around the country."

She opened her eyes and glanced at the sorceress. "Good."

"Kal, your eyes," Adele said when she opened them.

Kalliope conjured a mirror. Her eyes were two mini-suns. She gasped. The power receded and she went back to normal. She handed the mirror to Theresa. Seeing that only made her think of Lugh. Tears threatened again. She heard a loud crack of thunder outside that shook the building. Anna groaned.

"Not more rain. My pansies are soaked."

"How long has it been raining?" Kalliope asked.

"Almost two weeks, about the time you've been gone," Adele responded.

Kalliope felt the color drain from her face. She was having an effect on the weather. "How is that possible? I'm not Mother Nature."

"You don't have to be Gaia to be tapped into the weather. You're a sun goddess, babe, with the touch of the other elements because of your background. The rain isn't widespread. It's been real gray and the weathermen don't know why. You've gotta have a sense of how powerful you really are now. You surpassed me when Lugh healed you last year. Now you're up there. You can pluck a star from the sky if you wanted. You could go supernova and blot out part of the sun if you truly desired. You have to get a hold of your emotions. This isn't about being a witch anymore and you conjuring a rain storm. If you wanted, you could summon a hurricane and wipe out the Eastern Seaboard. No one is telling you to stop mourning for Lugh or forget about him, but you have to deal with it. That was the reason for the chocolates. I had to get you calm enough so I could reason with you, but you're taking this a lot better than I thought you would."

She drew in a breath and reined in her emotions. Letting her sadness simmer, she watched the sky lighten. The clouds didn't completely blow away, but rays of sun poked through the thin veil.

"I still can't believe it," Theresa commented.

"What do you mean?"

"Well, you're a goddess. We all started off being regular witches. Two years later, we can all do magick and you're a supernatural being. I thought I was going to freak when you pulled that rabbit out of thin air. Or when Apollo showed up when I was pregnant, but now this is all commonplace."

"It's mind-blowing, isn't it? Imagine how I felt when I first saw Merlin create a dragon from ash. Poor thing frightened the knights so bad they chopped its head off when it was only a baby. You get used to it." Morgaine shrugged and popped a truffle into her mouth.

"I'm not sure I'll ever get used to it," Kalliope whispered. She glanced at her coven sisters and the sorceress, feeling their comforting presence, but deep inside her something was broken. She couldn't dwell on it anymore. It was time to move on. Others needed her help. It wasn't good to have a demoness running around unchecked. At least no mummies had shown up yet.

At that moment, someone knocked on her door. She got up and peeked through the peephole. No one was on the other side. *Great*. Another knock. Everyone gathered behind her. She opened the door, and standing on the outside was a creature bound in linen bandages. She stepped out of the way and the figure fell forward.

"What the hell is that?" Theresa asked.

"I don't think it's the stripper we booked for today," Anna replied.

Kalliope knelt down and touched the figure. When she did, the bandages stuck to her hand. She realized then that it wasn't bandages, but webbing. She tore the webbing away, feeling her fingers getting numb. Underneath was Isis.

"What is this stuff?" Morgaine asked.

"Ginger's web. Be careful. Get too much of that on you, and it'll paralyze you."

The sorceress started cracking up. "Isis is going to be so pissed when she gets out of here. She's a bitch anyway, but man."

Together they kept taking off bits and pieces of the web. Kalliope tried to use magick on it, but the web was magick proof. They got most of it off the goddess. When they took the last piece from her face, she drew in a long breath and opened her eyes.

Chapter Eleven

"Where the hell is that no-good spider? How in the world did she get out? And where am I?" Kalliope felt the goddess gathering her power and was about to do something when her gaze settled upon her. "You! You let her out!"

"Who? Ginger?"

"Yes, Ginger. That no-good back-stabbing spider. Why did you set her free? She was exiled into the temple and made to serve Anubis for all time. I put up the wards myself and you released her!"

"How was I supposed to know she wasn't allowed to leave the temple? I didn't have a memory, remember? I had no idea because my powers were bound and there were a bunch of pictures on the wall. I guess she has some unfinished business with you. Why did you get dropped off at my doorstep?" Kalliope motioned for the others to sit back down. They watched while Isis came into the living room. She stopped at the border of the circle and glanced at the ceiling.

"Planning on trapping me? You think now that you're some hotshot goddess you can steal my powers?"

"Isis, will you shut the hell up for once? Kalliope didn't plan any of this. She's still mourning Lugh's death. She can hardly function. Cut the crap and tell us why you were wrapped up in a spider's web. The last I saw you, you were joking around with Nas and Flidais. Do tell so we can figure this all out." Morgaine sat in a chair by the coffee table.

"Are these *humans* going to be staying?" Isis asked. She conjured her throne and sat on the golden chair.

Kalliope rolled her eyes. She understood why Ginger had balled her up in webbing and shut her up.

"These humans are my friends. Where are Anubis and Ginger?" Kalliope asked. She was getting tired of listening to the Egyptian goddess going on and on.

Isis crossed her arms over her chest. Her midnight eyes met hers and didn't blink. This was going to be a battle of wills. She could do this. Kalliope returned her gaze and waited. Silence stretched out before them while the others sat. Isis's power flared out and tried to touch Kalliope, but that triggered the power of the circle and surrounded all of them, protecting them. Isis gave her a dirty look while a smirk turned on her lips. She couldn't help it if the circle had a mind of its own. She liked the fact the crystals were super charged now. Hopefully, the energy wouldn't burn the building down.

"We could do this forever unless you want to cooperate. I had nothing to do with any of this. I was on the edge of Summerland with my parents dealing with Lugh's death. If you cared about him in any way, please don't make this tougher on me than it already is. Don't you know what it's like to lose a husband? Or was Osiris's death another myth to placate the human population?"

Isis's energy died. All of a sudden, large drops of wetness rolled down the goddess's ebony cheeks. It seemed she had hit a nerve. She tried to keep her composure, but her head was in her hands, and she was bawling. All the other women glanced at one another. Morgaine shrugged. Kalliope grabbed a truffle and a tissue that Humphrey handed her and offered it to Isis. After blowing her nose loudly, she ate the truffle and hiccupped.

"Phank-*hiccup-hic*-you." She blew her nose again.

"Ahh, no problem. I didn't mean to, ahh, make you cry."

Isis waved her hand while she wiped her tears away and drew in a long breath. "No. It's okay. I try not to think of Si. I'm sorry about Lugh. I didn't mean to be such a bitch. It's just that I couldn't believe he would choose you, a lowly mortal. How could a glorious sun god fall for a humdrum human when he had me? And then he was dead. I was so mad at you for siccing the jackals on me. They weren't supposed to listen to you. I mean, how they could listen to you, a human, with no memory about magick? I was going to oppose your marriage, you know. I went to your shop and saw your humble life and thought, how could Lugh end up with this?"

Kalliope ignored the jabs, but inside, she was fuming. She wasn't about to get into it again with the goddess. Hearing her insults was one thing, but knowing she was going to deny her marriage was another. She had to get past all that and figure out what was going on because from what she knew, there was still a demoness out to suck up Anubis's ka. And she had no idea why David had been out of his body in the tomb with her.

"Isis, getting past all that, can you tell me anything about what happened after I left with Constance?"

"After the others calmed me down and confirmed that Lugh was dead, I took Anubis back to the temple. I don't know where Ginger went until she showed back up in the underworld temple and began spinning me into her web. She got me before I could do anything. From what I knew, David was playing poker after he was reunited with his body. Why is it so important that you know where they are? Once I find Ginger, I'll squash her. I should have turned her into a mummy when I had a chance instead of a spider."

"Why did you turn her into a spider? Was she going on and on that she was more beautiful than you?" Anna asked.

Kalliope figured Isis was appalled that a human was addressing her directly. She was ready to counteract any magick the ancient goddess was about to perform. No one was going to hurt her friends.

"You're thinking of Arachne. She was Roman and boasted about being a better weaver than Minerva. The Roman gods are a whole different bucket of worms than the Greek ones. It's bad enough they have to share Mt. Olympus. Stupid Romans never should have interwoven their pantheons."

Everyone glanced over to the new voice. Flidais stood in the hallway pulling out cobwebs from her hair and off her face. She appeared haggard and tired. Kalliope barely sensed her energy. Something was seriously wrong.

"Flidais, are you okay?" Kalliope caught her unsteady friend. She guided her to another chair that appeared in her already crowded living room. The goddess felt slight and frail.

"No. I'm not. Dagda, Nas, and the others are being held in the oak tree. Ginger webbed them up and has been feeding on us. She's going in order of who has less power and working her way up. Spiders are overrunning the oak and the forest. If you don't act soon, there won't be anything left of us."

It wasn't possible for one spider to do so much damage. How in two weeks could an entire pantheon of gods be taken down? Something else had to be going on. Someone had to be helping her. "Isis, do you know Ginger to be powerful enough to take over the whole Celtic realm?"

"No. She'd have to have help. How did you escape her web?" Isis asked Flidais.

"It was a fluke really. I wasn't completely wound up. Come to think of it, I remember hearing voices when I was suspended. I was in and out of it. I'm older than Dagda, so it took longer for the web to affect me. She was talking to another woman about souls. Something about how she needed more souls in order to break free completely. Do you know how that would be?"

"It's gotta be Ammut. She was the one after Anubis and me when I was in the temple."

Isis snorted. "Ammut doesn't have any power. She can only take the souls of those who weigh heavier than Ma'at's feather."

"So do those souls go to the Underworld? Does Anubis have anything to do with them? Why would she come after him? I was there when the screams of the ka were coming after him, and there was a woman in the shadows. He originally told me that you and he had broken up. Is that true?"

All eyes turned to the dark goddess. She cringed, but that didn't take away her inflexible demeanor. "Well…I…yeah, sure, I let Ammut off her chain and gave her a little extra power to get Anubis, but she wasn't supposed to go off by herself and try to suck the essence out of every god that she wanted. I…ah…only wanted Anubis to feel empty the same way I did. She wasn't supposed to kill him. Just suck his essence from his body for a little while."

"So you sent her to Lugh's bachelor party to kidnap him? What about David? How did he get in the mix?" Kalliope's temper blazed. *This bitch started all of this. What the hell? Can't she keep it in her own pantheon?*

"Take it down a notch, Kalli," Flidais warned.

She glanced over and saw the candles across the room were melting. Something plopped on her head and settled into her hair. She glanced up. The tiny bits of wax that had been stuck on her ceiling for two years were finally coming off. Maybe her power was good for something. Studying her friends, she saw that they had all broken out in a sweat, but weren't saying anything. Their trepidation was evident.

They were starting to be afraid of her. She never wanted that. Taking a deep breath, she pulled in her power.

"When I saw that he was going to the bachelor party, it brought back up a lot of feelings that I had for Lugh, which was why I looked closer at you and realized you were human. It was the best course of action because that demoness can't get to Anubis when he's in his temples or in the Underworld. So I blocked the way for him. It was either get him at the party or when he was at one of David's stupid poker games. And trying to get in there is like getting into Fort Knox. It was the perfect opportunity for me to scoop Anubis up and try to woo him a little bit. I told Ammut to have a little fun. She must've had a taste for David's sweetness and sucked him up. I'm not sure why he ended up in Anubis's temple."

"I'm sorry that you got dumped, but that doesn't mean you had to pull me into your internal squabbling. Your stupid test got Lugh killed. How does that make you feel?" She pushed past them and into her bedroom. She slammed the door and sank onto the bed. *This isn't happening. Because of that harpy, he's dead.* Tears began to fall onto her dress, but it didn't matter. The sun was shining outside.

The goddesses knocked on the door, but no one could get in because she didn't want them to. After all of this was over, she was not going to be dealing with Isis ever again. She had to focus and figure out how to stop Ginger and Ammut. So far, she assumed that the spider didn't know that she knew she was onto her. She had to play it safe. Someone had to have brought Isis to her doorstep, but who? *I have to figure this out. I can't let the others get hurt. I can't let Dagda have the life sucked out of him, even though it is a thought, and Nas doesn't deserve that. What am I going to do?*

"Need some help?"

Kalliope felt the added weight to the bed. She glanced over and saw her familiar reclining on the pillows with his legs crossed. "How did you get in here?"

"You might be a goddess, but that doesn't mean I'm not still connected to you." He puckered up his lips for a kiss.

She screwed up her nose at him. Frogs might have grown on her, but she still had trouble with them. "No kissing, Humph. And yes, I need some help. I need you to go and see how bad it really is in the oak tree. Can you do that without getting wrapped like a mummy?"

"And what do I get in return?"

His question startled her. "What do you want? A companion?"

He hopped over to her on all fours. "I want my freedom."

Sadness entered her heart. He would leave her too. "Aren't you happy?"

He nestled against her chest and sighed. "Oh very…ribbiit. But I want to be able to come and go as I please and not be tethered to you. I'd still hang out with you, if that's okay. I don't want to be your pet. I'm an independent frog and I want to sew some of my froggy oats."

"Okay. You help me resolve this thing, then I'll let you go your merry way, but you have to promise me something."

"Anything, babe."

"Okay, two things. Stop calling me babe, toots, honey, pumpkin, whatever. We've had this conversation before. And I'll set you up with your own lily pad, but you're still going to babysit because the twins love you."

He stuck out his webbed foot. "Deal."

She scratched between his wings and shook his hand. "Deal." A zap of power passed between the two of them, sealing the pact.

"How do you feel about being hairy and having eight legs?" Kalliope picked him up. She imagined him being a spider before he could protest. His white wings grew into four other legs. His body elongated and got brown and hairy. Staring back at her with twelve eyes was her familiar.

"You turned me into a spider, didn't you?"

"You do like to eat flies. Don't get yourself caught. Whatever you'll see, I'll be able to see too. Now get going."

Humphrey jumped down off of the bed, wobbling on his new four legs. She stifled a laugh when he crawled up onto her bureau and kept checking himself out in the mirror. His long fangs made her shiver. He wasn't as big as Ginger, but he would be able to take on the small spiders.

"I like this." He waggled his bushy eyebrows at her. She wasn't sure how he ended up with those.

Kalliope waved her hand over the mirror. The scene changed to the lush clearing that she had first encountered when she stepped into the other realm. Now, what was reflected was completely different. The trees were covered in cobwebs so thick they were layered upon one another. Some of them had crystallized. The sun reflected off the spider webs. The trees were alive with all different sizes of spiders. Cocoons from tiny to huge were stuck to the trees. The pond was covered with a web. Along the outcropping of rocks, she saw a cocoon with an arm hanging out of it. A shriveled one that she recognized. Whatever Ginger had started, she was truly sucking up the life from the realm. If she didn't act quickly, there would be nothing left. Kalliope had some unresolved issues with Dagda, but she couldn't let the world that Lugh loved so much be eaten away by spiders and an Egyptian demoness.

The Sacred Tree was in the distance. Leaves had fallen around its base and there was a large hole where the recarving wall had been.

"Get in there and be careful. If you can, try and get Nas and Dagda free. Tell them to come here."

"How am I supposed to do that?"

"Why do you think you have those fangs? You cut through the webbing. Now hurry up and don't get caught."

Her familiar blinked at her with his numerous eyes and then jumped through the mirror. Once that happened, she closed the portal between the worlds and watched him skitter along the webbed grass. She observed him until he was out of sight and prayed that he wouldn't get caught. Now she had to figure out where Anubis was and get him away from Ammut.

Chapter Twelve

The knocking got louder. She dropped the barrier around the room and let the others in. Theresa was the first one that entered. Her coven sister gasped when she saw the image of the clearing. The others followed. Kalliope took her friend and hugged her. She didn't want her to be afraid.

"I'm sorry about before. I didn't mean to lose control. Having all this power is mind-blowing. It feels like I'm going to burst at any minute, and I'm all warm and tingly. You have to be feeling some effects of this since we're all tied together and everything."

Her friend nodded. "I didn't want to talk to you about it in front of the others, but yeah. We're all feeling it. It makes me lightheaded. Are you going to be okay with all of this?"

She smoothed her friend's hair and saw the concern there, but also saw how frail Theresa was. She was human, and something was going to eventually kill her, no matter how much magick she had, unless she ended up taking up on Avalon and living her life out there. Either way, thinking about losing her friends now was not a good thing. With the extra magick, they would have longer and fuller lives. Kalliope was glad they weren't afraid to face the future.

"Honestly, I really want the drama to end. I'm tired of getting mixed up in all these magickal debacles."

"Where's Humph?" Anna asked.

"I sent him into the other realm for recon. I was hoping he could get an inside view into what's really going on. I turned him into a spider."

"Wow, I'm impressed that you could think of that." Isis rubbed her red nails on her skirt to clean them up.

"Shut up, Isis!" Morgaine and Flidais said in unison.

Kalliope glanced at the other goddess and saw that she looked a little livelier, but not by much. Hopefully, Dagda and the others were faring okay. "Flidais, how did you escape? You never said, just that you were not as tied up. Do you remember?"

They all turned to the other goddess. She sighed and put her hands on her hips. "You know, I don't know. The last thing I remember was hearing the spider and another woman talking. Then there was a black blur. Things got clearer when I was in the hallway. I started coming around. Someone must have pulled me from the tree. I'm sorry, I don't know who."

Kalliope nodded. *Okay. There's a stranger helping them somewhere along the line. Just as there was in the desert. Abbas mentioned a woman. I thought it was Isis. But there was another woman that was looking in the window at me the first time I met Isis. And in the window when Corrine was hurt.* Thinking back on her, she realized she was calmer and more peaceful than Isis had been. *It was Isis who offered for me to go with her. It had to be. But who is the other woman?*

"I think she has something to do with all of this." Kalliope recalled the other time she had seen her watching in the shadows when Ammut was coming after her and Anubis.

"What are you going to do about it?" Isis asked.

"I'm going to look for her. Flidais and Morgaine, can you take queen bee and go search for Anubis and David to make sure they're okay? We have to make sure that Ammut hasn't gotten to them."

Flidais and Morgaine looped their arms through Isis's. She began to protest, but Flidais shot her a look. A bolt of power moved between her and the other goddess. Kalliope nodded. The three of them disappeared, leaving her coven behind.

"What do you want us to do?" Adele asked.

She faced the three witches. Over the past three years, they had grown with her in power, but she didn't think they could grow anymore. It seemed magick was already bursting from their eyeballs. She didn't want to disappoint them, but in case Ammut or Ginger came after them, they wouldn't stand a chance.

"I want the three of you to get the twins and then go to Avalon. You don't want to get mixed up in this. It's dangerous."

Theresa scowled. "Are you saying that we can't handle ourselves now that you're some hotshot goddess?"

"No. I'm not saying that. It's…I know how to handle these situations better than you do. I've had more experience with gods. Please, if they get a hold of you…" She started to cry again, thinking what her world would be like if they were gone. Lightning illuminated the sky. "Sorry. You're the only family I have left. I can't lose you too."

"Fine, but we don't like it. We'll go to Avalon and see what we can do from there," Anna added her opinion. All three of them joined hands and held out their arms to Kalliope. She was still their high priestess and commanded the circle. She smiled. Once their hands connected, the power between all of them came to life. A great blast of energy shot upward. It was so strong it broke them apart. Kalliope opened her eyes to find she was sprawled on the bed with her dress over her face. She smoothed her dress back to find out what they had conjured. Inside the circle was a large pumpkin.

"How did we get a pumpkin? I wasn't wishing for anything. You guys?" Theresa asked the cousins.

They shrugged, and when they did, the pumpkin moved. It broke into three different orange balls. The balls unwound, and instead of the pumpkins, there were three orange cats with large brown spots on them so when they were put together, they had looked like a jack o' lantern. Kalliope giggled. She scooped up one of the fluff balls and it began to purr. All three kittens meowed together.

"Oh my God! Kitties! They're so cute. How—"

Kalliope let go of the struggling cat and plopped it on the bed so it could head off toward Adele. "They're not just cats. They're your familiars. Guess the universe decided you were ready for them."

"I'm allergic to cats." Anna backed away from the kitten coming toward her. Kalliope picked it up and put it in her friend's arms.

"You won't be allergic to her. You might even get them to talk. We can figure it out later. Interesting. Please take them back to Avalon with you. We can discuss how non-catlike they'll be." She glanced at the cat in Theresa's arms and saw its lips turn up in a smirk.

"You may fool them into thinking you're cute, but I know what you really are. You had better watch them and keep them occupied. Is that understood?" Kalliope said to the cat.

It meowed its response.

"I'll be back. Get the twins and get to safety. If you don't, I'll know." Kalliope waved her hand and sent the three of them back to their apartments. Each of them had enough magick now to open a gateway to Avalon. Theresa knew the way best, but the rest of the coven had been there before.

She closed her eyes and followed the link between her and the frog. He was creeping up the Sacred Oak and searching for a more discreet way to get in without being noticed. Ginger was in the center of the room with her fangs stuffed into one of the cocoons. Kalliope pulled back and shivered. It was time for her to act, no matter what the cost. First, she had to find Ma'at and see if the goddess could help her.

If I were a goddess, where would I be? Oh wait. I am a goddess and I'm standing in my bedroom. Lame, Kalli, really lame. I have to focus. God, Lugh, I wish you were here right now. I could really use you to work off some tension. That and I just need your help.

She took in a deep breath and thought about what she knew of Ma'at, which wasn't a lot. In the past, she'd never really gotten into the Egyptian pantheon besides Isis and Osiris for major deities when she cast a circle. *Well, I know now I'll never call on Isis again. Who would ever think she was a stuck-up bitch?*

What she knew of Ma'at was that she weighed souls. If they were lighter than the feather, then they passed on to their heaven. If they were heavier, then Ammut devoured them. So she was a figure of balance. Kalliope snapped her fingers and thought about the goddess. A book appeared in her hand. She glanced through the entry based on Ma'at and saw that she regulated the stars, seasons, and the actions of both gods and humans.

Maybe that was one reason she was watching what Isis did to me. Maybe she was seeing that it was fair. I don't know. I have to find her, though. She has to help me with Ammut.

Glancing down at her clothes, she envisioned herself in jeans, hiking boots, and a T-shirt in case she ended up stuck in the desert again.

Oh heck. I have no idea where she is. Best start with the last place I saw her.

Kalliope willed herself back to the village, but this time, she didn't want the villagers to see her, so she was invisible. The sun beat down on the top of her head. She craned her neck to see if she could detect a dark spot in it that had been Lugh or if a plane was passing across it. She did admit now that as she focused on it, she felt the intense heat of the orb, but it wasn't burning. It was above her and inside of her also.

Pulling herself back to her task, she walked to the well and peered into the darkness. Seeing the blackness, she saw how far she had fallen. She shivered, remembering her trip into the water. *I never want to do that again.*

Backtracking, she made her way to Abbas's house. Immediately, she felt horrible about Corrine. The woman had tried to help her, and she had run off. Again, she had no choice because her husband had been calling her a witch. She wanted to be sure that she was all right. Quietly, she stepped into the shade of the home, but didn't see the mistress of the house.

"It's you!" A gasp and the sound of something breaking made Kalliope turn around. Corrine stood in the doorway. Kalliope realized she could understand her now thanks to her magick. And she could see her.

"Please, I won't hurt you." She bent down, gathered the shards of the water jug together, and willed it back together. Even the water was inside of it. Corrine took the jug and then set it down inside the door.

"I'm not afraid of you. I was just startled, that's all. Wow, you can understand me now."

Kalliope nodded. "I wanted to apologize for when you took me in. You were hurt because of me. I wanted to return and see if you were okay."

Corrine smiled. "I'm fine. My husband is afraid of things he does not understand. Most people are. I knew you were different when Abbas brought you here. I didn't know how to tell you. Language barriers suck, but you're not just here to see if I was okay. You're looking for someone."

"How did you know that?"

Corrine touched her hand and closed her eyes. "You've lost someone very close to you. Someone that was part of your soul. You should not despair. All is not lost. You seek one of the old gods. I can show you where she resides, but I would ask for one thing in return."

Kalliope wasn't sure how to respond. The more she studied her, the more she realized that this woman was something of an oracle, a psychic. Her inner being glowed with a purple light. It was more than her aura. She saw Corrine's spirit. When she stared into the purple light, she sensed other beings standing watch over her, guardians, angels. Kalliope focused on one of them, seeing a tan, dark-haired woman with a loving smile and large gray wings. The being nodded at her, but before she could acknowledge the angel, her perception returned to normal.

The flash forward was a little unnerving, but whatever Corrine wanted, she would grant. She was a special person that needed the protection. If her husband ever found out the extent of her abilities, Kalliope wondered if he would call her out and say she was a witch too.

"What do you want? If I can make it happen, it's yours."

Corrine smiled. "I want a child. Abbas and I have been trying for many years now. I believe that because of my peculiar abilities, I'm unable to conceive. Can you give me this? I know you are a goddess and that the others would never believe me if I told them this. Many think I'm a sorceress, but they don't take action against me because my husband is a powerful man in the village."

Kalliope sat down, unsure how she was going to make the woman have children. *Do I have that kind of power? Lugh and I had talked about children and he said that we didn't need to worry about kids because we both had to really want it. I don't even know where to begin with my power, but I have to try.*

Corrine waited for her to say something. Kalliope smiled and shut her eyes, still seeing the purple light of her hostess before her. She stretched out her senses, examined the color a little more, and saw there was some kind of blockage. It was a black spot in the middle of her aura, a tumor. Kalliope reached out, surprised to find her hand passed into the light. She was able to hold onto the blockage and pull it out. Corrine gasped. The bright light of her power flared along her arm and burned up the dark spot. In her vision, she passed her hand over the place that was now empty and channeled some of her energy into the hole to replace it. When the rift was sealed, she backed away and opened her eyes. Corrine had her hand placed over her stomach. Tears slid down her cheeks.

"Please tell me I didn't hurt you? I didn't mean to. I—"

"No. No. You did it. I felt it. It wasn't my abilities. It was something worse, wasn't it?"

Kalliope nodded. A wave of relief went through her. "It was a malignant tumor. You should be able to have a whole gaggle of children."

Corrine threw her arms around her. "Thank you. I'll be forever indebted to you."

"No. Honestly. Let's call it even if you can show me where Ma'at is. I don't want to be revered for anything."

Her hostess nodded. "There's an ancient temple I go to when my husband isn't around. It is nearly buried by the sand, forgotten by all others, but I found it. It's a beautiful place. Only it's a half a day's walk from here."

"I don't have that kinda time. Think of the place in your mind, and I'll bring us both there."

Corrine closed her eyes. Kalliope held the woman's hand. Once she connected to her, she could see the image also. Power flared around them, and they moved forward. The woman gripped her hand, but they reappeared in a matter of seconds outside of a large sand dune. When

Kalliope examined it closer, she saw it was a cave that the sand had covered up.

"Come on. I'll show you." Corrine motioned her forward.

Kalliope studied the vast desert around them. There was nothing else out here. If there was, it had been reclaimed by the desert the way so many other burial grounds and temples had been. She would've loved to have seen Egypt in its heyday. Maybe when this was all over, she would see if she could time travel. It would give her a break after everything that had been happening to her.

She trudged through the sand and into the coolness of the cave. Once inside, she saw the walls were carved with intricate hieroglyphics honoring Ma'at. She saw the pictures, but could also understand the words too. This was so much better than when her power was bound. Many of them were tales of the goddess and how she weighed souls, but there was also another passage that said, "Main temple this way." Kalliope smiled. This was exactly what she needed. When she began to move into the cave, she sensed the stirrings of magick ahead.

"Corrine, you can't go any further." Kalliope saw the old candle stubs and incense from the altar she had set up and still used.

"I know not to. There are old, powerful magicks ahead that I don't understand. I can barely make out the words on the walls, but I understand them. She enjoys when I sing. I don't see her all the time, but I feel her hovering and listening. She was the one who told me about the herbs I used on your legs when you came to the house."

Kalliope was stunned that Ma'at was communicating with Corrine. It seemed Ma'at was aware of what Isis was up to. "Well, I hope that she can help me. If not, I'm not sure what else I can do. Thank you for bringing me here. I'm glad that you're okay."

"I hope that we'll see one another again. I think you'd be fun to hang around with." Corrine hugged her.

"We could have a blast. Think of home, and I'll get you there."

An image popped into Kalliope's mind. She sent her new friend back to her house. It was sad to see her go, but it was good to know that she was okay, too. *I hope there are no more mummies in this place. I could really do without any more shrunken people coming after me.*

Following the ancient direction signs that kept saying, "this way to temple," or, "turn left for temple," she wound deeper inside the cave. The further she went, the heavier the magick got. It was also pitch black. To solve that problem, Kalliope conjured a mini-sun that revolved around her while she walked to give her a good view of the corridors. She came to a dead end. Before her was a large scale painting on the wall. On the left plate was a white feather. On the right was nothing. To the right side in the distance was a picture of Anubis. To the left was a picture of a female figure with a crocodile's head. Ammut. Her teeth appeared to be sharp, and the painted red eye was watching her every move. The magick she sensed at the mouth of the temple was the strongest here. Kalliope saw two different realms. One was the human world where a secret button had to be pressed and the wall would spring open. The other was the entrance to Ma'at's temple in the astral realm. However, she couldn't pass.

"Before you can enter, you must be weighed." A booming voice echoed around her.

Great. Just great. The stone began to shake, and dust fell from the ceiling of the cavern. She jumped back, watching the scales come out of the wall. The gold scales grew larger. The floor fell away before her, and the two balancers were even with the floor. A small feather sat on the left panel. *There's no way I'm going to weigh less than the feather. I know this has nothing to do with weight. It has to do with the measure of conscience and soul. With everything that's happened, I have no idea what's going to happen. Wouldn't it be hilarious if I end up being snacked on by Ammut after all?*

Kalliope took a deep breath, knowing she couldn't hold off the inevitable. The longer she delayed, the more at risk the Celtic realm became, and she couldn't let any of her friends get hurt. She stepped onto the gold platform and held onto the two chains. The floor behind her fell away. She held on for dear life as the blackness beneath her stretched outward. A large pair of glowing red eyes leered down at her. The scales began to sink. The platform shook more. She glanced at the other side where the feather was nearly touching the top of the scales. The scales started to rise. Her heart lifted some, but then it went back down.

Kalliope closed her eyes, feeling her stomach drop as the scales quickly went all the way down. They stopped with a thud. She clutched the chains. Her heart sank then. It seemed that she wasn't found admirable in the eyes of the goddess. The eyes above her narrowed.

"You have been judged and found unworthy. You will be sentenced to an eternity of purgatory."

"How is that fair? I've given my life for those that I loved."

"You've also used your power to hurt the other gods, nearly killing them. You've used your magick to take advantage of the universe to have things go the way you want them to."

She hung her head. That was true. She had hurt the others when she lashed out after losing Lugh. Events in her life did end up going her way when she needed them to, but it wasn't deliberate. When she first met Lugh, she was nearly broke, but after he appeared to her, luck changed. Her bank account filled up from orders for her candles that she'd now grown into a shop. "It wasn't intentional. I was heartbroken. I just lost the man I loved. I was reacting to the loss. And I never purposely manipulated the universe to make things go my way. I hate to cast spells. I do things the mortal way if I can. Please, I'm trying to save my friends. If you can't read my true intentions then what qualifies you to be a goddess?"

"You have no right to judge me." The scales stopped moving.

"I'm not judging you. I'm only saying that I know it was you who dropped Isis at my front door. I know it was you watching outside of Abbas's house. I know you were there watching Isis be her cheerful self at the store. You can't be helping and then pull away. What kind of balance is that?"

"That is exactly balance. I do not take sides. I am here. I have always been here and I shall remain."

"If that's true, then why has your temple fallen away? Humans don't remember who you are except what they see in museums. Your places of worship have long since crumbled. I know what that means. Soon it will mean that you will fade. If there's no belief in you, then there is no goddess," Kalliope yelled into the darkness. "The only reason you've gotten more powerful of late is because Corrine has come here and lit candles for you. She prays to you."

Hot air blasted all around her. The scale lifted up once again. It stopped when it was in perfect balance with the feather. "And what about you? What happens when no one believes in you anymore?"

Kalliope pressed her head into the chains. There was only one thing that she wanted. "Then I get to see Lugh again. I'd give up the magick, the coven, whatever it took, if I could hold him one more time. I never wanted this. I just wanted him." A tear slipped from her cheek and landed on the platform. When that happened, she was elevated up and she was lighter than the feather. She sniffled and wiped her eyes. The floor returned. She jumped down from the scales and faced a throne. A woman wearing a dark veil and dark dress studied her. Gold earrings dangled from her lobes, and intense eyes watched her.

"Now you have spoken from your heart. You have been judged worthy of what you seek."

"So it was you helping me all along?"

Ma'at stood up. "It was. I have lingered here for a long time, dwindling away as you have said because humans do not believe. Isis did not think I had enough power to make myself known or control the demoness. That is why she loosened Ammut onto Anubis. Unlike her and the others, I choose to dwell within the mortal realm. That is why my powers are so weak. Once Isis let loose Ammut and gave her more power, there was nothing I could do to stop her. Now I fear she is even too powerful for me."

"So what happens if you can't control her? I need someone to call her off. She won't listen to me."

"I am the only one who can control her. Isis was a fool to think she could've."

"Will you help me get her back here so I can save the other gods?"

Ma'at nodded. "I will assist you, but we will need some backup. I don't know where Anubis is, but his pets will be able to find them."

"The jackals."

"Yes. They're loyal to no one except him. I suggest you go there first and ask them for aid. Once they sniff him out, he and I can take on Ammut. His rule also extends over her because he can choose the ka she swallows. Do you mind if I tag along?"

"Of course not. I would appreciate it." Kalliope visualized the temple where she had encountered the jackals.

At once, she was whisked away, with the other goddess at her side.

Chapter Thirteen

They reappeared in a large temple. Once they did, they immediately saw the jackals were snarling and snapping at something. Kalliope ran around the throne to see what they were going after. Huddled against the back of the throne was Flidais. The beasts sensed Kalliope's presence and stopped. Once they did, the leader yipped and wagged its tail. The others didn't let up on their attack.

"It seems you have a way with animals. The jackals do not take orders from anyone else," Ma'at commented.

Kalliope patted the jackal and glanced at the cowering goddess. Parts of her arm were bleeding where the beasts had taken chunks out of her. "All right, you guys, you can let her go. She's a friend of mine."

The jackals looked at their leader, who growled something and then backed away. The others followed. Flidais got up and dusted herself off. "Thanks, Kalli. Those jackals sure are mean."

One of them growled.

Kalliope chuckled. "Where are Isis and Nas?"

"Spiders got Nas. We were in the forest searching for David, following poker chips. We came to the end of the trail and found him strung up in a web. He had this horrified expression. I've never seen him that way before. His signature deck of cards was on the ground and there were spiders all over him. Nas tried to free him, but our magick is dwindling. The spiders overpowered her. Isis and I got away, but we heard this screaming in the shadows. I looked behind me and all I saw were these faces and dark ghosts.

In the middle of them were red glowing eyes. I sensed teeth. It was coming for me, but Isis pushed me out of the way and sent me here."

Kalliope's heart sank. Nas was captured. David was strung up and waiting to be eaten. *I wonder if that's a cheesecake god's worst nightmare.* Isis was sucked into Ammut's jaws. Anubis was still unaccounted for. If the jackals didn't find him and Ma'at and she couldn't deal with Ginger and Ammut, then all would be lost. "Okay. Well, we are all that's left to save them. Are you up for it?" she asked both of them.

"I'm almost out of magick, and soon you'll start feeling the effects of it too, Kali. You're a Celtic god since Lugh gave you his godhood."

She nodded. "I know, but I'd rather go down burning than just flaring up and piddling out. Ma'at, you in?"

The other goddess nodded.

"What about you guys? Will you help us find your master?" she asked the jackals.

The leader stepped forward. When he did, he morphed into a man with tan skin, sharp claws, and deep brown hair. The others followed suit. "Whatever you desire, mistress."

"Alrighty then. I didn't see that coming. Are you his personal guard?"

"We have hidden our true forms from those who do not understand our master's position. We protect him, and if need be, protect the Book of the Dead, for it is a powerful object. It can bring any being back to life or condemn them to limbo."

"We don't know where Anubis is, so we need your help. Can you find him for us?" Ma'at asked.

"Of course. We will take you to him now." He scooped Kalliope up and flung her onto his back. She snuggled into him, piggyback style. The others did the same and carried the goddesses on their backs. The world moved by faster while they ran. She didn't notice where they were going except she sensed the sensation of magick upon her skin, tingling everywhere it touched. They stopped and the world came back into focus. When it did, they were standing before a poker table.

They hopped off the jackal warriors' backs and approached the empty table. Anubis was shuffling cards. The last time Kalliope was here had been when he and David were in a poker tournament with several others. He flipped the cards nervously and kept them moving. His guards got to one knee and slapped their fists in a closed hand salute on their chests.

"Master, we've brought the red-haired one to you as you had commanded."

"Thank you. Please return and guard the Book of the Dead."

The warriors bowed their heads and morphed back into jackals. The leader rubbed up against Kalliope and gave her a smile before running off to rejoin his comrades. She smiled warily. *Why is it that the strangest creatures find me attractive?*

"Do you really think this is the best time to be playing cards when you're needed?" Ma'at huffed.

He growled. "I'm not playing cards. I've been waiting for Kalliope to get here so I could take action. I couldn't let Ammut get me, and this is the only place besides my temples she can't enter."

Kalliope nodded. Isis had said that she wasn't able to come here and get David, so it was logical that the god would come here also. "Well, here I am. Will you help?"

Anubis rose. "Of course. First—"

Before he could say anything, one of the jackals returned and bowed. He was out of breath and bloody. "Forgive me, master."

"What is it? Where's Niran?"

"It was the demoness. She came out of nowhere. She overpowered us and took the Book of the Dead. Niran was sucked into her maw. The others tried, but I was the only one to escape. I have failed you. I give you my life."

"Enough! I'll have no talk of that. You have been honorable. I will recover the book. Stay here with the women and guard them."

"Whoa! We're going with you."

Anubis shook his head. "It's much too dangerous. If you're caught, Ammut will suck you up too. I have to get the book back. No one else can use it. If they do, they could wreck havoc on the Underworld. Only my power can control it."

"I have to go. I can't let the others be dinner or dessert for Ginger and her spiderlings. I don't care. Why would Ammut want the Book of the Dead?"

He shrugged. "I have no idea. Ginger has been barred from the lower temple for eons because she was caught in the chamber that houses the book. Isis exiled her at my command after she turned her into a spider. I've always been good to her. She hates Ammut. Why would she be getting involved with her?"

"Do you know how to free the gods from their webs?"

"Fire. She's afraid of it, and it will burn through the web. You just have to get to her before the web touches you."

Kalliope nodded. She could do fire. "Great. Let's go."

"Take my hand, ladies."

All of them touched the god. Kalliope drew in his musky scent and wished that it was Lugh. He was warm and full of life, but for how long, she didn't know.

They arrived in the center of the oak tree. The inner core of the tree was blanketed with hanging cobwebs. Around the wall were a hundred cocoons. On Dagda's throne sat Ammut. Her eyes were red and her skin was a pale green. She had three taloned fingers and pointed teeth. Spiders covered the walls, and Ginger had made her home at the crown of the tree. Her web spanned the entire top of the tree, several hundred feet across. Kalliope knew that she hated spiders for a reason.

"My, my, I was wondering when you were going to get here."

All of them spun around. Standing at the entrance of the tree was Isis decked out in all her regal garb. Her hair was perfectly straight with a golden crown nestled upon her head. At her throat was a large golden torque that resembled wings. Gold bracelets hugged her upper arms. She wore sandals that laced around her calves. Her eyes were lined with heavy makeup and her lips were bright red. She was the complete goddess that Kalliope had always envisioned and seen depictions of. Her presence demanded she bow, but she wasn't about to.

"Isis, you're okay. I thought Ammut got you," Flidais exclaimed.

The other goddess chuckled. "That's what I made you think. Foolish, Flidais. You've always been a little blonde for my taste. It's a shame, really, because you're one of the older goddesses left. You and I, we used to be so close." She sauntered past them to the throne and petted Ammut on the head. The demoness gawked at her with admiration. Kalliope's stomach turned. She'd known something was off about Isis from the first time she came into the shop.

"Isis, what is this all about?" Anubis asked.

The other goddess gazed at the death god. "You should know what this is about. It's always been about the same thing." Opening her arms, Isis said a word Kalliope couldn't understand. Before them appeared a large black sarcophagus. On the other side of it was a table that contained four jars, an ancient book, and a golden ankh nestled between two candles. The effigy of a man was carved on the top of the stone coffin. His hands were crossed over his chest, and he wore a serene expression. The magick radiating from the casket almost knocked her to her feet.

"You can't tell me that this is about resurrecting Osiris again? Do you remember what happened last time?" Anubis asked, and stepped toward Isis.

The goddess giggled. "Of course I remember. Why do you think there are thousands of mummies lying under the sand? We performed the ritual and the mortals were suddenly inspired to mummify the dead. They came up with this whole system that got a little out of hand. I mean really, did they need to start mummifying their cats and place their dead servants in the tombs with them? All because this ceremony didn't work."

Anubis almost made it to Isis, but Ammut stood up and growled. Kalliope watched her eyes deepen to blood red. The demoness opened her mouth, but Isis put a hand on her shoulder. "Leave him, dear. We need him. Why don't you snack on the others?"

"No matter what you do, the rite won't work without me. Even if I do it, you don't have all of Osiris's parts. That's why it didn't work the last time. Isis, leave him be. He's been resting peacefully for all these centuries. His time has passed. Why can't you be happy with me?" He placed his hand on her cheek. Anubis truly loved the goddess. She understood that kind of love. A pang of longing stabbed her heart.

Isis gazed at him lovingly, and then her expression twisted into one of disgust. "Did you really think after all these years of me sleeping with you that I was doing it because I enjoyed it? Please. Fucking you was like humping a lowly dog. I only did it to learn some of your secrets, which I appreciate you sharing with me. It's amazing how naïve men truly are when you have them between your legs."

Anubis snapped at her.

"Now, now. I can tell Ammut to suck you up too. Maybe I'll have Ginger wrap you up in her web."

Kalliope felt something tickling her leg. She glanced down and jumped. All of Ginger's children were crawling over her feet. She hadn't noticed before, but when she tried to move, she was stuck. Her toes were tingling from the effects of the web. The other goddesses were trapped too. Ginger descended from above them and was easily walking over the webbed grass.

"I thought you hated Ginger?" she asked Isis.

Isis turned her attention to her. "Oh, I did. But we worked out our differences a long time ago. She was the one who originally told me where the Book of the Dead was. Then Anubis caught her and exiled her from the lower temple. Thanks for getting her past the barriers he put up, by the way. Because of her working so well with Ammut, I have enough power to resurrect my dead husband. I'm sure, Kalliope, that you'd love it if I also brought back your dead lover. Lugh was amazing in bed, but he never lived up to Osiris. Alas, I won't have enough power, and I never really liked you anyway. Ginger can bind you and then Ammut will use your power. It will be added to the others so I can pull Osiris back to me. She and her children will feast on your bodies."

"You're such a bitch. Ammut, it's time to go. Come to me," Anubis commanded.

The demoness sauntered over to Ma'at and kissed her cheek. "You don't own me anymore. Our queen has given me enough power. I don't have to be chained to your throne. I am free."

Ma'at chuckled. "You only think so. Once this whole show is over, Isis will use your power too. Your existence will end. You won't be anything. Come back to me and we can forget this ever happened."

The demoness opened her mouth and placed her lips only inches from Ma'at's. The goddess tightened her grip on Kalliope, but before she could react, she wilted to the floor, a shrunken husk. Ammut wiped her hand across her mouth and smiled. "She was a little dry for my taste. I've wanted to do that for such a long time. Who's next?" She stepped toward Kalliope and Flidais.

"Leave them be for now. I want them to watch those they love end up like Ma'at. Once I'm done, then you can have them both."

Isis walked over to the sarcophagus and slid the lid off in one push. It crashed to the floor and cracked into several large pieces. The tree shuddered, and branches fell from above. All of them were dead. Lying inside the onyx coffin was a mummified man with a scream frozen on his lips. Kalliope saw a large gold chest plate resting on his chest. Gold and silver rings adorned his fingers. The power from the coffin almost bowled her over.

The demoness licked her lips and pushed Anubis to the other side of the coffin. Isis took her place at the head of the coffin with Ammut on the left side and Anubis on the right. She took the tops off the canopic jars and then lit the candles. The ankh glowed in the light. The goddess opened the book.

"It won't work, Isis. You can't pull him back."

"Shut up, Anubis. I don't need you to do anything. Just be here. All it takes is your presence. I know all your secrets, and with you echoing my words, it will come to pass. Osiris will rise again, and we will have a new age of wonder. Shall we begin?"

Ammut closed her eyes and stretched out her hands. A glow began to emanate around her. Kalliope felt a tugging from deep inside of her. She glanced around and saw the cocoons were glowing too. She glanced at Flidais and saw she was growing paler. Her gaze scanned around the tree.

A flash of blue caught her eye. *Excalibur*. Beside the sword was a rather large cocoon.

"Dagda?"

There was a glimmer of response. Consciousness, but no words.

"Come on, Dagda. I need you to wake up. I need your help."

Again, she didn't get a strong response. He'd been wrapped up in the web too long. Kalliope felt more tingling on her legs and saw the spiders had worked up to her knees. The glow from the cocoons was blinding. All of the power was focusing into Ammut, who breathed out. While she did, the glow began to encompass the jars. The contents of the clay containers floated upward and settled over corresponding parts of where they had been removed from the body. Isis had the Book of the Dead between her hands and was reciting the words in Egyptian. Anubis swayed back and forth, caught in a trance. His hands were lifted also. Flidais leaned on her, ready to collapse.

It was all up to Kalliope.

Chapter Fourteen

Kalliope watched the organs settle back into the body of the dead god. The energy Isis was siphoning from the other gods now glowed inside of Osiris. The skin on him began to plump back up and appear lifelike once again. Excalibur flashed. The connection between them flared to life. *Fire.* Anubis said fire would cut through the webs. She blocked off what was going on around her and focused on her power. When she did, she found that the sun power inside of her had shrunk. Ammut was also siphoning her power. Plus, the web was up to her knees. *I can do this. I know I can.*

She envisioned all of her energy surrounding her in fiery whips. All of the whips were hitting the walls and burning through the webs. Immediately, she was warm but not hot. When she opened her eyes, her entire body was on fire. Spikes of flame whipped around her. Wherever they touched, the webs shriveled up. The screams of the spiders came to her, but she didn't bother with them. The fire seared through the webs along her feet, and she was able to move. The longer she blazed, the quicker she was feeling the drain of her own power.

"What do you think you're doing?" Ginger hopped before her, trying to stop her, but she wasn't getting too close.

"Making sure this doesn't happen. What Isis is doing is wrong. You should know that. Besides, I thought that you hated Isis because she turned you into a spider. Don't you want to be human again? Don't you hate her for what she kept from you, from all the years that you could've been with a man? Help me out. If you do, I'll make you human again."

Ginger clapped her fangs together. "Kalliope, I don't remember what it's like to be human. I am what I am. And Isis and I made up a long time ago. I was her best friend back in the day. We could never be separated. When all this is over, I'll rule this realm. It will be a wonderland for me and my children."

Kalliope glanced at the fires and saw the webs falling away from the side of the tree, revealing the gods underneath them. Many of them were shriveled, but she sensed the life in them. She had to act fast. She switched her attention to Isis. Both Ammut and Anubis swayed to the chant that Isis recited. The being in the coffin now had long, dark hair. The gold ankh pulsated was power. A beam of it was now focused on the head of the fallen god, filling his facial features. Osiris's dark skin shone in the candlelight, and he was handsome.

"You won't rule anything!" A fireball left her and engulfed the spider. A loud scream filled the tree. At that moment, the other spiders also cried out. Her energy was dwindling. She had to stop this.

"Excalibur, come to me." She summoned the sword to her.

The sword began to worm its way from the web, working toward her. After another moment, it flew into her palm. Once her fingers wrapped around the pommel, she felt her clothes change into warrior princess garb again.

One of these days, you and I are going to have a long discussion about what you dress me in.

The sword was amused, and she noticed it was not affected by the power drain. That was a good thing. *Glad you think it's funny because right now, we've got some work to do. Hope you're up for it.*

The blade grew warmer, and she noticed her power wound down the blade and made it light with fire. Some of the other gods were beyond resurrection, but Dagda was coming around. He still wasn't in any shape to assist her. She walked to the end of the coffin. Osiris opened his eyes. His dead stare fixated on her. His fingers flexed and slowly gripped the side of the sarcophagus. A chill ran down her back.

"It's working. Ammut, we need more energy. Pull in all that you can. Ignore everyone. Osiris, my love." Isis reached toward her rising husband.

Kalliope felt her energy being sucked on even more, but she had to keep going. She raised Excalibur and pointed it at Osiris's heart. If she threw the blade, it would hit its mark. The blade knew her goal. "Isis! Stop this now or Osiris will be no more!"

"You! Aren't you dead yet? I can feel your energy wavering. Soon, you'll be a dried up shell. Your energy won't last forever."

"I might be losing my power, but my aim will be dead on. Do you really want to take that chance?" She pulled back her arm. The sword hummed while it waited to be thrown. It had been her ally one other time in the past and helped her free the world from an overbearing god. It was time for her to save the gods she cared about once more.

Isis didn't make any move to stop. Kalliope was growing weaker, but she couldn't let on. Osiris was breathing and stirring more. He blinked. There was light in his eyes. He wasn't dead anymore. His ka, his essence, had been summoned back from the Underworld. A pang of longing went through her. She didn't want to do this. Osiris had nothing to do with what Isis was doing, but she knew that raising him was not the right thing to do. He had been dead for so long that it would throw off the balance in the world. Anubis was correct. It wasn't something that should be done. Isis had to be stopped. She understood that love had driven the goddess to be desperate, but her grief had also driven her insane. She didn't want that to happen to her.

"Don't make me do this, Isis!" she warned the goddess. Osiris flexed his fingers and began to move. Kalliope felt her knees wobbling. Her throat was dry. The flames were no longer whipping around her. She was almost out of power. Ammut opened her mouth wider, if that was possible.

Kalliope turned and threw the sword straight at the demoness. Excalibur hit his mark, straight into her open mouth. The impact toppled Ammut to the floor. The glow was suddenly cut off from the ankh and the one that surrounded Osiris. Isis screamed, but Osiris was sitting up in his coffin. Isis rushed to him and wrapped her arms around her resurrected husband.

"My love. You came back to me."

Kalliope's heart sank. It was too late. The god had been revived. His dark eyes didn't leave Kalliope's. He cocked his head and gazed at her. His fleshly body begin to disintegrate in his wife's arms.

"No. You can't leave me. You can't. Not after all of this."

His eyes were the last thing to become lifeless. All the time he didn't break his gaze with Kalliope. When the light died in his eyes and he was only a pile of dust, she heard a faint whisper echo into the fading light.

"Thank you."

She understood that Osiris didn't want to come back either. He was happy where he was.

Isis wailed. When she did, the ground beneath Kalliope began to shake. She stumbled and fell backward onto her butt. When she tried to get up, something came up through the grass and grabbed her foot. It was a hand. Glancing around, she saw the cocoons falling from the tree. Dagda was stumbling around. Flidais was still passed out on the floor. Anubis was still locked in his trance.

Another hand broke from the dirt and grabbed her foot. Kalliope tried to summon her power, but she was at her breaking point. Darkness threatened her vision. Ammut might have been dead, but she was running on reserve. She reached out with her mind and called Excalibur to her.

The sword vibrated from the ashy remains of the demoness and then it was free. When it came to her hand, its power ran up her arm and gave her the strength to swing at the hands. Moans erupted behind her. She swung the blade and severed the arms that were around her hand and ankle. Isis was rocking back and forth, holding powder in her hands.

Getting up slowly, she heard the cracking of bones, but they weren't hers. Dozens of mummies were stepping out of the walls of the tree. All of them moved slowly, advancing toward her with blank expressions on their leathery faces. She swung Excalibur around her in a circle. Where the blade touched their dried skin and linen, they turned to ash, but the more she chopped through, the more came. There was a never-ending stream. More hands pushed thought the dirt, along with faces.

The mummies slowed, but she kept cutting them down. Anubis was finally out of his daze. "What happened?" he asked.

"You were helping Isis. Can you get these guys off me, please?"

Anubis said something and waved his hand, but the mummies didn't disappear. "I'm not sure what's going on."

"You're the Lord of the Underworld. Make them go back into their crypts."

"I can't. I don't have any power. Ammut drained mine as well."

"Wonderful." Kalliope struck more mummies that were heading toward her. The only one way to make this stop was to confront Isis. The goddess was crying, her cheeks now stained with Osiris's remains.

"Isis, call off your mummies. I don't want you to join your husband."

The goddess looked up and hopped off the edge of the sarcophagus. "You wouldn't dare kill me. I'm too established for you to kill me."

"Does it really matter? Your followers forgot about you ages ago. The majority of the kingdom that worshiped you is under the sand. You don't belong in the forefront of everyone's minds. All Hail is the only one that has the majority of the rule."

"I don't care about ruling over the other gods. I only wanted Osiris back, and you made that impossible. Now he can never come back. He's gone. And you're going to pay!"

Isis launched herself at Kalliope. When she did, she changed into a large vulture with sharp claws. Kalliope dove out of the way and rolled on the floor. Somehow, she avoided the mummies, but she noticed the other gods were coming to her aid. She got up and swung the blade at Isis, but the goddess dodged. Kalliope watched her wing around the top of the oak tree. The goddess spread her wings out in an eight-foot span and dove. Kalliope lifted Excalibur, blade side up, but the goddess wrapped her talons around the edge of the sword. She didn't let go of the handle. Isis shrieked. A blue arch went between the blade and her talons. The goddess rose up and circled.

An image appeared in her mind. It was the sword, but broken up into smaller throwing stars. There were six of them. Kalliope knew from experience that her aim would be true, guided by the sword's otherworldly power. She felt a shift in the air and the sword's power shimmered over her. When she glanced down, she was dressed in a black outfit from head to toe. She could only see from a slit where fabric didn't cover her eyes.

"Seriously?" she asked the sword. *"Now I'm a ninja. When did this all happen? Were you watching Kung Fu movies with Dagda?"*

The sword didn't answer. Instead, it shifted and she was holding six throwing stars that all glowed blue. Isis screeched again. She drew back her arm to throw the first three. Before she let them go, a hand came down on her shoulder.

"Please, don't kill her," Anubis requested.

"Why shouldn't I?"

"Because you really don't want to. And because I love her."

"She was a bitch to you and nearly drained all your power. She set Ammut on you. She's nearly destroyed the Celtic realm. Not to mention she wanted me dead. Wouldn't it be easier if she were out of the way?"

Anubis shook his head. A mummy reached out to grab him. Their hollow moans were getting on her nerves. The death god waved his hand, said something, and the dried up corpses disintegrated into dust. "I know what she did to me and to you, but even if she doesn't feel the same about me, I still love her. Besides, there's no one else strong enough in our pantheon to carry out her punishment. I don't want All Hail stepping in and deciding what will happen to her. He'd only make it worse, and he doesn't understand. Please."

Kalliope glanced at Dagda, who was holding Flidais and clearing away the cobwebs from her hair. He nodded. "It's for the best. Your obligation to him is complete. Besides, he'd owe you one in the future."

"I don't care if you owe me one."

Isis was circling all of them and keeping her distance. Kalliope thought about only getting the edges of her feathers, but not piercing her flesh. Excalibur was disappointed, but when she threw the first batch of stars, they landed on their marks. The stars pinned the vulture to the wall at various parts of her body. She screeched and transformed back to human form. Kalliope could see the blades were only centimeters from her flesh, caught in her gown. If she moved the wrong way, the power of the sword would kill her.

"Why don't you kill me?"

Kalliope saw the anguished expression and knew that was what the goddess wanted. She called the blade back to her. All the stars came together and then formed a sword before settling back into her hand. Isis fell to the floor. She rose and adjusted the torque on her neck, trying to appear dignified.

"Here, Kalli. Use these to bind her." Morgaine was behind her with a pair of silver shackles. The same ones that Hephaestus had forged and, when worn, no magick could be done in them.

"Is everyone in Avalon okay?" she asked.

The sorceress nodded. "The spiders got several of the priestesses, but they're okay, thanks to Humphrey. He was the one who warned us. I almost didn't recognize him as a spider until he started touching my breasts with his hairy feet. You have to teach that frog some manners."

Kalliope laughed and took the chains. She walked over and saw Anubis trying to console Isis, but she didn't want any of it. He stroked her hair, but she kept trying to pull away from him. "Isis, you're going to go with Anubis, and he'll decide your punishment." She took one of the goddess's wrists and tightened the shackle around it.

"Why didn't you kill me?" she asked again.

Kalliope sighed. "Because I saw what I could become holding onto Lugh. I can't do that. So in some sense, you're a reminder of that. And, I feel for you. There's no excuse for what you did, but any woman hurt by love would understand. Before you go, you have to know this." She put the other manacle on. "Osiris was happy where he was. He didn't want to come back."

"Liar! He would have wanted me to revive him. He loved me."

"Maybe he did, but somewhere deep inside, you know what I'm saying is true. Think about it." She nodded at Anubis to take Isis away.

"I'll make sure she's taken care of. I think she needs care more than punishment until she's back in her right mind."

Kalliope nodded. Anubis took the chains and led Isis out of the oak tree. Kalliope sheathed Excalibur and asked the sword to go back to Avalon for awhile. She figured it would end up back at her apartment. It had a way of doing that no matter how many times she left it with Morgaine. Once they left, Kalliope walked toward Dagda and felt her remaining energy drain away. Excalibur had been lending her its strength, and now it was gone. She tried to make it a few steps, but Morgaine caught her.

"Thanks."

"Why don't you rest? I think we can take it from here. You've done enough, Kalli," Dagda reassured her.

Chapter Fifteen

Kalliope wasn't sure how long she slept in Avalon, but when she opened her eyes, she felt a little better. Her energy was low, but the atmosphere around her was full of life. Even after all the events of late, a deep hole remained in her heart. She gazed at the red engagement ring Lugh had given her. It was the only reminder she had left of him besides his power. She thought back to him on the edge of Summerland and wanted to hold him at least one more time.

Thinking about her ring reminded her of Isis and how easily she could turn into the goddess. She couldn't obsess about wanting to bring Lugh back, even though she understood that it wasn't possible. She had to move on with her life. Her coven was there for her. The other gods were there for her. She had friends and family. The twins would need a loving aunt to watch over them and teach them how to use their magick. Her coven would need a high priestess to use their magick.

She rose from the bed. When she did, she was dressed in a white shift with a silver pentacle at her throat, silver bracelets on her upper arms, and rings on her other fingers. There was a slight burning between her brows. When she studied her reflection, she saw the blue upturned crescent of Avalon. She drew in a sigh and walked out of the room. A full moon hung in the sky. Silver light shone down and hit the circle of stones, radiating outward and touching the priestesses who were worshipping on the Tor.

"Amazing seeing it from this vantage point, isn't it?"

Kalliope glanced at Morgaine, who was beside her in the doorway. "Yeah. It's awesome. I remember when you had me in the circle, and I freaked out when the energy hit me. Who's leading it?" At that moment, something twined around her feet. Looking down, she saw the three cat familiars her coven sisters had conjured. It was good to see they were safe.

"Theresa. Adele and Anna are both in it too. I thought it'd be good for them."

Kalliope chuckled and wondered how the girls were dealing with the influx of all the magick. "I'm sure they'll handle it well enough. So, how long have I been out?"

"A week actually."

"Seriously? I didn't think that was possible."

"You're a goddess, my dear. Things are a little different for you. How are you feeling?"

Kalliope stretched. "Tired still. I need more time to recover. Thank you for letting me stay here."

Morgaine put her arm around her. "You're always welcome here. Humphrey is waiting for you." The sorceress walked away and headed toward the Tor. Kalliope sighed and knew that she had a promise to keep to her familiar.

She turned and stepped back through the door. The air moved, and she was in her apartment. Humphrey sat on the sofa watching television, reclining on his back, his legs crossed. He blinked his eyes at her.

"Oh ribbbii-it. Aren't you a sight for sore eyes."

She giggled. "It's good to see you too, Humph. So, what do you say, you want to be a spider forever?"

He scrambled and jumped over at her. She noticed that he had gotten the hang of using his webs. "Please turn me back. I'll do whatever you want. You can take back the deal that we struck."

She laughed. "You are *way* too overdramatic." She snapped her fingers and instantly, her familiar was turned back into a frog. "All better?"

The frog glanced down at himself, patted his froggy body, and unfurled his white, feathery wings. Once he was airborne, he did a little dance. His antics had her in hysterics. She leaned on the doorway and laughed until her sides ached. It had been a long time since she had laughed that way.

"Thank you. Thank you."

"Come here, you big frog. I made you a promise." She grabbed him by the sides and brought him to her lips. The frog puckered up and she kissed him. At that moment, something snapped inside of her. Humphrey was now free. She hoped that he wouldn't completely leave her. "You can do whatever you desire now. The clearing you went to is open to you. I do need you to do me one favor when you get there, if you don't mind."

"Anything, my love."

"Tell Dustbunny, the goblin who lives there, that the fairy queen wants to go out with him. If he says yes, I'll send him a hundred pairs of mismatched socks."

"I would be honored." Humphrey flapped his wings and then winked at her. Once he did, he popped out. Sensing his absence, she sighed and glanced at her apartment. There was cleaning to do. She could easily do it with her powers, but Kalliope wanted to do it the old fashioned way. The human way.

After cleaning and scrubbing, she headed to the store to see what was going on there. Hopefully, nothing was wrong or no one had tried to break in. Willing herself over there, she appeared in the back room by the closed door. When she did, she heard a loud shriek. Right before her was Chase. He threw the feather duster up in the air and grabbed his chest.

"Where in the hell did you come from?"

Kalliope bit her lip. She hadn't realized that Chase was minding the store. "Ahh… I ahh…came in through the door. I didn't know that you were here." She patted him on the shoulder. "Sorry. What are you doing here anyway?"

"I've been watching the store for you, silly, while you've been away. How was your trip? Did you get some sun and sand like you planned?"

She sighed. If only it was vacation. "Not really. Thanks for taking care of the place. Is there anything that I need to do?"

He glanced around. "No. Nothing. I've kept the place clean the way you wanted. Your shipment of crystals came in that you ordered. The other girls left a list of what needed to get done. So you can hurry along and get back to that big luscious hunk of yours."

Kalliope tried to smile, but hearing that only brought back the memory of seeing Lugh dying in her arms. The need to hold him once more time came over her, but she brushed it off. That couldn't happen ever again. "Thanks, Chase. I appreciate you looking out for the store."

He beamed. "That's what friends are for. Scoot. I got it covered. Anna is going to be coming in tomorrow to be sure."

She gave him a quick hug and then walked into the front of the store. No one was there, but she could still feel the echoes of the ka that had invaded her space. The new crystals hummed with a life of their own. She ran her hand over all of them and infused them with her power. It took her a little bit longer, but when she was done, she could see that inside of the five crystals was a mini sun. When triggered, the crystals would form a barrier inside the store that none could breach. The energy would last forever or until the quartz shattered the way the others did. Envisioning where she wanted them placed, she sent them into various parts of the store. These would do for now, and later, she would place smaller crystals around the store to spread out the energy, just in case.

Everything else was in order, except she did notice that her inventory was low. That meant she had to get cracking on making the candles and bath salts. She would do that the old fashioned way, too. It wasn't any fun willing them into existence when making candles had always been cathartic for her.

Chase was still dusting in the back room and the closed sign was on the door. The moon was full, but she didn't feel like going back to her house. She was in the mood to roam. Her thoughts took her back to the glade where she had first conducted her Lughnashin ritual. It had been the coming of summer, and she had been so excited only to have her radio struck by lightning and melted. That was when Lugh had first appeared to her, called by the loneliness in her heart and the fire the strike had created. Then, whenever fire was around, he came.

The glade was the place where Flidais had married her parents. It was the place where the twins had their Wiccaning. So many things had happened there. Magick had seeped into the grass and into the trees. It was a place between the worlds that was only slightly apart from the human world.

"This place has a lot of memories for you."

Kalliope didn't bother to meet her Aunt Constance's gaze. She sensed the ghost a fraction of a second before she appeared. "You know it does." She stared up at the moon, feeling its silvery power flow into her. It wasn't the same as when she had been human. Before, it would prickle her skin, but now the cold light seemed to war against the sun energy inside of her.

"You can't change the past. I'm sure you learned that with Isis."

"I did. And don't worry, I don't intend to try. I was just reminiscing. It helps with the pain."

"What will you do now that you're a goddess?"

Kalliope met her aunt's eyes. She sensed the woman had an ulterior motive for being there. She hadn't just come to see if she was okay. "I don't intend on trying to take over the world or any other realms, if that's what you mean. You can tell All Hail that I enjoy my life the way it is. I don't want his job. I would think after everything I've done that He would know that."

"I had to ask. You do have Excalibur and all."

"Don't worry. I don't want to screw up my chances of seeing Lugh again whenever I die. So go back and reassure him. I really don't need any more hassles after what I've just been through. Forgive me, but I'm not up to being put under the microscope."

"Kalli, I'm sorry about Lugh. You know that. Would it be okay if I stop by and make you a pie sometime?"

She instantly felt bad for snapping at her dead guardian's ghost. She gave her a quick hug, smelling the cinnamon and nutmeg that clung to her aunt even in death. "Any time. I'm sorry. I'm still tired from the whole Isis thing."

Constance smoothed her hair. It made her remember that when she was a child, her aunt would do that before she went to sleep. Her songs used to drive the nightmares away. She wasn't sure that would ever happen.

"You know tomorrow is Samhain. It would be a good idea for you to pay homage to those who have crossed on. Your parents, Lugh, anyone else that you might want to. You'd be amazed at who can hear you on the night of the dead."

She patted her cheek and then backed away. "I'll do that." Kalliope knew she was telling her something, but she wouldn't figure it out until it actually happened. *Maybe she's saying that I can see Lugh. One night even, or one more minute. That's all. I want to say goodbye.*

Her aunt nodded and then faded out, becoming one with the rays of the full moon.

Chapter Sixteen

Kalliope spent the rest of the night and most of the day making candles until she ran out of supplies. Sleep had eluded her no matter how much she tried to settle down after she got back from speaking with Constance. Her mind raced about what was going to happen. Samhain, Halloween to the rest of the world, was a powerful holiday when the veils between the worlds were the thinnest. Sprits walked the earth. Dead relatives gave messages to their loved ones. Sometimes, humans danced with otherworldly beings and never suspected anything was wrong. She'd always loved the holiday. For her, it was the ending of one year and the beginning of a new one. For children, it meant haunting neighborhood stoops until someone came to the door to fill their pillowcases with candy.

When she had been a child, Constance would make her think about what she wanted to be for the next year because in her beliefs, whatever she dressed up as was what she would embody for the coming year. Most of the time, she ended up being a fairy so she could frolic and have fun the next year. Sometimes, Constance let her get away with being a ghost, and most of the next year, she was practically invisible to every one of her teachers.

Standing before the mirror, she envisioned herself in a witch costume. A black hat appeared on her head with the point lagging off to one side. A skin tight black dress materialized that showed off her curves with a ruffled skirt that revealed her shapely legs. Those were encased in white and green striped stockings. She had ankle high granny boots on to match. A small beauty mark appeared on her left cheek. Her red and black hair was piled under the hat and fell out from under the brim in waves. She put her hands on her hips, pleased at what she saw. *Lugh would've loved this.*

Before she could get sad, there was a knock on her door. When she didn't open it, she heard the key turn in the lock and the doorknob hit the wall. At that moment, her air conditioner kicked in. Pots rattled in her kitchen. She stepped out of the bedroom and saw Adele, Anna, and Theresa carrying the twins and ransacking her cabinets.

"And what do you think you're doing?"

They stopped. "Ahh. Nothing. Just getting some stuff for the party that we're having later." Adele turned red.

"Party? What party?"

"Wow, don't you look the part?" Anna said.

Kalliope eyed the three of them. Something was up. "Not that I mind you coming in here and taking advantage of my self-stocking cabinets, but what is going on?" Theresa was about to touch the bag she had on the counter. She snapped her fingers, and it reappeared on her coffee table.

"Hey!"

"That's off limits."

Theresa stuck her tongue out at her. "That's all you had to say. No need to get feisty. For your information, we're heading to Avalon. Morgaine and the other priestesses are throwing a huge bash. All the gods are going to be there, including our dates. We were hoping that you would come."

"Dates? I thought I told you not to get involved with gods."

"They're demi-gods, and we like being involved with them. You can't tell us who to date and who not to." Adele stuck her chin out.

She threw up her hands. "I know. You take whatever you want and have fun. I'll be there after. I have something to take care of first."

Her coven sisters nodded. Kalliope didn't like that they were dating gods only because she didn't want to see them get hurt. None of them had to have their hearts ripped out the way hers had been.

She took the bag into her bedroom and laid out the contents on the bed. Inside were a basket, flowers, wine, sausage, cheese, and chocolate. All of these were offerings for the departed. She arranged them in the basket, and then willed herself to her parents' graves.

Dark clouds glided over the full moon. The night had an eerie chill to it. Spirits clung to graves and wailed when they saw her. Death was not her department. She didn't listen to their forlorn cries, but walked over and sat before the headstone. The glossy marble reflected the moonlight. She ran her fingers over the engraved names. She pulled out the flowers, some of the chocolates, and the some of the cheese.

"Thank you for watching over me all these years. Thank you for being there and comforting me when I needed it the most. I know it was all you were allowed. You have one another, so you're happy. Take care of him for me. I'm sure you will, but don't let him get the best of you. He likes to play tricks sometimes." She sat in silence and took in the surroundings. It was quiet and peaceful. The life around her wasn't moving because it was all dead.

She felt the moon rise higher in the sky. If she focused inward, she could see the earth floating like a marble in space. If she pushed her thoughts further, she could connect to other suns in other galaxies far, far away. Kalliope wasn't ready to test her vast power and see if she could travel to these other places. She was content with her life on earth and her friends. After getting up, she placed one of the flowers on top of the gravestone, leaving it as a final token to her parents. There was only one other place for her to get to before she joined her friends.

She gathered her offerings and willed herself to Avalon, but not the Avalon where her friends were celebrating. To the one she was connected to, the place that was the threshold of the dead. When she arrived, a light fog hung in the air. The gray lake was still. A light breeze blew through and stirred the reeds. In the distance were the remains of houses and the stone circle. She saw a fire through the clearing in the woods.

Taking the basket over, she uncorked the wine and poured some on the ground. "For the spirits who are thirsty and wish to drink." She cut a piece of the cheese and sausage and placed it on the ground. "For the hungry ghosts who desire to taste." She left the chocolate. "For those who yearn to experience the sweetness of life once again." At that moment, a large sigh went over the place. A whoosh passed over her, and she grew cold. When it disappeared, her offerings were gone.

"I haven't felt the spirits this appeased in a long time. You have given many of them peace to be remembered."

She turned and saw the fey queen standing before her. "I hoped that they would be. I wouldn't want anyone to not be remembered. Not even in this place. I'm sure you've seen hundreds of ghosts pass through here to the other side."

"I have, but tonight seems to be different. Not many goddesses come here. I think that even the lords of the dead may have been summoned by your display. You may want to give them your attention now. You'll come to the celebration after with Morgaine?"

Kalliope glanced over the lake and saw a figure gliding over the water. "Yeah. I plan on it."

"Good. Then I'll see you later." The fey queen disappeared.

A cold chill stirred up on the land. The mist thickened. The figure was coming closer over the lake, but she realized that it wasn't gliding. It was flying. Large black wings flapped close to the surface of the water, making it appear to be a large raven in the moonlight until it settled on the ground. When it did, Kalliope was met with a skeletal face and bony fingers. A tattered black robe hung on the figure's body. A deep shiver went through her soul. This was Death. It wasn't Charon, the ferrymen of the Greek underworld who shuttled souls of the dead. This was Azrael, the angel of death.

He pulled back his hood. At once his face disappeared and was replaced by a handsome pale one. Deep black eyes reflected the universe and stars. He smiled and bowed. When he did, she saw his pointed canines, marking him for an otherworldly creature more so than what he already was.

"Good evening, Kalliope."

"Hi," she whispered, trying to hide the fear she felt from his presence.

"There's nothing to be frightened of. I haven't come to harm you. Nor do I think has my brother Anubis." He held his hand out to the other god.

Kalliope turned and saw the jackal-headed death god holding a large book under his arm. The same book Isis had stolen. The Book of the Dead. He grasped Azrael by the elbow and then turned his attention to her.

"How is Isis?" she asked.

He shook his head. "She's no better. I am afraid that I might have to keep her with me forever. The chains have made her tolerable, but she still blames you for what happened to Osiris. I have tried to tell her that Osiris didn't want to come back, but she forced him to. That was the true reason the ritual didn't work. He might have been whole in body, but dragging him from paradise was not what he wanted."

"Well, I hope that he's back where he wants to be." She noticed the fog was thicker than it had been before. Power was building in the air. *Why are they here?*

"He is. That brings me to why we're here. Do you know why we're here?" Anubis asked.

"Because I paid homage to the dead spirits. Because it's Samhain. Because—" She didn't want to say more. She couldn't think about it.

Azrael took her hand and kissed her fingers. His lips were silky. "Your love for the fallen god is almost as bright as the power inside of you. It's blinding, but ever so much worth it. I know how it feels to experience that kind of love. It got me through the darkest time in my existence. Because of my mate, I don't have to be alone. No one deserves to be alone."

Kalliope's eyes widened. Could it be possible? "I thought you said he couldn't come back. That it was wrong to resurrect a god? How can...?"

Anubis opened the book in his hands. After a moment, it floated in the air. "I owe you a boon. You saved my life when you killed Ammut, and you stopped Isis. I can't completely bring Lugh back from Summerland because it's not my domain. I can do the summoning spell, though."

"I can escort his sprit back because I was the one who took it, but there's still one problem," Azrael told her.

Her hope swelled. They were saying it was possible. "What problem? What can I do?" Her tears fell onto the grass, and she saw white starflowers appear.

"We need three things," Anubis answered.

"What?"

"We need a piece of his flesh, his willingness to come back, which we already have, and the magick that made him a god," Azrael answered.

Kalliope began to panic. "I don't have any of his flesh. You can have the magick."

Anubis touched her hand. "You have a piece of his heart, don't you?"

She glanced at her ring and understood. It was a piece of him. "Yes." She took it off and gave it to him. "Here. What do I have to do?"

Anubis said a word, and a stone table appeared before them. He stood at the head. The book hovered above it. Azrael was on the right and she was on the left. The death god placed the ring on the table. He then raised his arms and began to chant. The redness of the ring began to grow and pulsate until it was the size of a human heart. Kalliope was stunned as she watched the event unfold before her. Anubis's chants were in a language she didn't understand, and she wondered if it was the language of the dead.

The jackal's eyes glowed green while the moonlight caught the glint of the golden ornaments he wore on his arms. Azrael was the complete opposite next to him, swathed in silver from the moon and a dark purple aura that pulsated. Power built until it crackled around the god. The angel of death withdrew a golden orb from his robe. Kalliope felt Lugh's essence, his soul. Azrael placed it over the pulsating heart. For a moment, nothing happened.

"Will you give your blood so it will flow within his veins?" Azrael asked.

She glanced from the heart to the angel and nodded. Before she could protest, he grabbed her wrist and tugged on it. With sharpened nails, he sliced open her vein and squeezed. She bit her lip and didn't cry out. Her blood dripped onto the heart and pooled on the table until it pulsated. While it beat, veins stretched outward, twisting and branching out until they were the length of a man. Anubis sped up the rhythm of his chant. The golden glow moved from inside the heart to along the veins until there was substance and that formed a body. Within the glow was the man she knew. Once he was a solid form, Azrael let go of her hand.

Kalliope noticed that he licked the blood from his fingers. She didn't comment. All her attention was focused back on Lugh. His golden eyelashes were curled slightly. The bridge of his nose was evenly spaced. His lips were the soft, full ones she remembered. His muscles were sculpted in all the right places, and his other parts were identical to what they had been before. She held her breath and waited for him to open his eyes, but he didn't.

"Why isn't he waking up?"

"Because he needs that spark of power that will make him whole," Anubis answered.

She understood that he needed his godhood back. "What do I do?"

"Lean over and kiss him. Will the power back into him," Azrael instructed.

Kalliope glanced at the both of them and blushed. She would have rather done this in a more intimate setting, but beggars couldn't be choosers. Brushing his copper hair out of his face, she placed her lips on his. He wasn't cold, but he wasn't warm either. He was always warmer than her, and she knew that was because of his power.

Closing her eyes, she envisioned the golden power inside of her spinning around and around until it condensed into one small, powerful ball. With everything in her, she released the power and willed it into him. She pressed her hands into her sides from the burning pain that crept up her throat and then over her lips. Once it touched Lugh's lips, he pressed his mouth against hers and swallowed the orb. His arms wrapped around her, and he began to pull more power from her. She didn't fight him, but let him take what was left of his god power inside of her. He let her go and collapsed back onto the table.

She stumbled backward and took in a deep breath. She was very cold. The luster of Avalon had vanished. She saw the dead grass under her feet and the lake of nearly frozen water before her. Anubis and Azrael hadn't changed. They only appeared larger than what they were. The jackal-headed god said one last thing. A beam of light came down from the moon and hit Lugh in the chest. It became so bright she blocked her eyes. Then the light hit her. She fell to her knees and tried to catch her breath. Once it left her, she had to hold her arms and try not to shiver. It seemed part of her was gone.

"What was that?"

Anubis said something, but all she heard was a growl. *Odd.* Her gaze trailed to Azrael. The angel had a peculiar expression on his face. There was a pressure on her mind and then he said something to the death god.

"It seems that Lugh needed a little bit more. We had to give him a piece of your spirit to anchor him in his flesh. I think we might have pulled too much out."

"What does that mean?"

"It means, love, that you have no more magick."

Kalliope's heart stopped when she heard his voice. Her eyes slowly turned from the dark angel to him. Lugh was sitting up on the table and gazing at her with bright green eyes. He was alive.

He hopped off the table and landed soundly on his feet. When he did, the Book of the Dead fell to the table and slammed shut. Anubis said something else, and then she felt him disappear. Azrael whispered something in Lugh's ear. He didn't break his gaze, but nodded. He reached out and took her hand. A zap went through Kalliope. Azrael smiled and then stepped backward into a dark rift. Then he was gone.

Warmth began to filter into her once more. Lugh had on a pair of black leather pants that fit every curve. He wound his fingers through hers and pulled her into him. *What was it he said about magick?*

"I said that you have no more magick. Anubis had to take it all to give me that little push for me to be back with you."

She reached out, almost a little afraid to touch him. "I'd forgotten that you can read my mind. Does it bother you that I have no more magick?"

He kissed her forehead. "No, Kalli. My brave, beautiful goddess. No matter what you are, you're the woman I love. Human, witch, or goddess. You gave up everything to bring me back. I watched you take on Isis and battle the others. No one has ever stood up to her. You saved all of them again. And this time, no one asked you to do it. You're noble and put the cares of others before yourself even though your heart was shattered. I'll never want anyone else but you."

Tear streamed down her cheeks. He was here. In her arms. He was alive. She threw her arms around him. His scent was of warm autumn leaves and deep pine. His body was hard against her. She couldn't stop the tears from falling. All she wanted was to bury herself in him and not come back out. Losing him had torn her apart, but now that he was back, she wasn't sure if this was some kind of dream and if when she woke up he would be gone.

His fingers ran up and down her back, feeling every bump in her spine. They wound through her hair and began pulling the pins that held the strands in place. Once they were down, he threw the hat on the ground, letting her locks tumble over her shoulders and down her back.

"You're alive. Oh God, you're alive. Please don't ever leave me again. I don't think I could bear it. I don't know how I did it when you were gone. I saw you when I was with my parents on the edge of Summerland, but I couldn't go to you."

"I saw you too. I wanted to go with you, but they wouldn't let me rejoin you. I wasn't sure if I ever could, but here I am. I didn't want to leave you. Please don't hold it against Dagda. It was an accident. He didn't mean it."

She nodded and rested her forehead against his. "I know. I don't. Not anymore. I forgave him. I couldn't let him and the others be drained. But when I saw Isis and what she became, I didn't want that for me. I was getting used to the idea that I wasn't ever going to be happy again, but here you are."

Lugh laughed. There were tears on his cheeks as well, but she didn't know if they were hers or his. It didn't matter. She was getting over the shock of him being resurrected. He was with her. "I'm sorry to disappoint. Although, I don't think that we can take back the magick that brought me back. I can call back Azrael, he and I go way back, but I don't think he will be able to oblige me on this favor."

"Don't call him. I don't want anyone else around except you. I missed you. I love you." She realized something and then started laughing, which turned into a bout of hiccups. He backed away from her a moment. "You know, I should be furious with you."

He gave her a questioning look. "And why is that?"

"What am I going to say to the others when they ask me where my engagement ring is?"

He smiled and caught her up. "You're haven't changed, my little minx. I'll give you the moon to wear on your finger if you want, but first, I think you owe me something."

"And what would that be?"

He snapped his fingers and then they were falling.

Chapter Seventeen

Kalliope landed on something soft. She didn't mind the stomach-dropping sensation and then the sudden landing. It was something she had grown accustomed to over the years. She got up from the bed and looked around. They were up high with a mountain view. Below them was a lush green valley that flowed into a tall and dense forest. The room she was in was nothing but windows. The sky was dotted with stars and the moon full. To another side, she saw more mountains, and one so high the top was covered by a skirt of clouds. She assumed that was Olympus. The height was a little daunting, but she didn't mind.

She glanced around the room and saw there was no ceiling, but she didn't feel the air above them. A large, canopied bed with flowers hanging down sat in the center of the room. Their perfume filled the space. She noticed a long hallway and wondered where she was.

"Do you like it?"

"Where are we?" she asked.

"I created this for you. I was going to take you here on our honeymoon. I thought you might need a place away from everyone where you and I could be by ourselves. Here, I'll show you." He took her hand and brought her over to the middle of the windows. He pointed to the mountain with the clouds. "That's Olympus. So if you ever feel like kissing Zeus again, you can."

Kalliope giggled, more aware of his heat radiating against her skin than anything. "I don't think that will be happening anytime soon. Ew."

Lugh pushed the hair off her neck and slid his fingers along her skin. She tried not to shiver. His hand came around her waist and set on her stomach. He pointed to the valley of trees. "There is our forest." He sent a zap of power through her. Kalliope curled her toes and squeezed her thighs together. "It's bigger than it appears, of course, but from way up here, it seems tiny."

"Mmmhmm." She bit her lip to keep from crying out as a result of a stronger blast of energy. Stars exploded in her vision. She wasn't going to let him get the better of her yet.

"Beyond the mountains is the Egyptian realm. The river that flows through the Greek realm and the Egyptian one are the same. It touches upon our realm, too." He kissed the back of her neck. "You taste so good. It was agony for me when I couldn't hold you when you were grieving. I think I drove the other spirits nuts, and that was another reason All Hail let me come back. That and he owed me a favor." He nipped her right ear and then trailed his tongue along the side of her neck.

Kalliope balled her fists, fighting the pleasure running through her body. She had missed this. The pain and longing from not being with him had all but vanished from her soul. Now she was rejoicing in being in his presence once more. But he was driving her crazy with his soft touches. She figured he was doing it on purpose. "What favor was that?" she managed to ask.

Lugh slipped down the shoulder of her costume and kissed along her collarbone. "I forgot how good you taste. A mixture of apple and nutmeg. Must be all those pies Constance makes you." He removed his other hand from her stomach and began to unzip her dress. "I reminded him how you had saved his butt. He can be quick to forget things. That and he had lost a bet to me in a poker game one time.

So I decided to call in my bet. You think I made a good choice?"

He slipped the dress from her body and cupped her breasts from behind. His nimble fingers rolled her nipples around until they were erect and hurt. Lugh squeezed them gently until she moaned and ground her bottom against the hardness that poked against her. Her toes were starting to hurt from being curled for so long. She couldn't remember a time where their lovemaking had been this intense. Maybe the first time. It was always mind-blowing, but this was different. He was taking his time with her and not overwhelming her with sensations.

"Don't you know I want to worship you, Kalli? Every minute of every day, I'm your slave. No one will ever harm you again." He read her mind.

Her head fell back against his chest. She peered deep into his eyes and saw him smile. His lips met hers in a small kiss until he began to deepen it. Kalliope ran her tongue over his lips and touched his. Their tongues caressed one another until she pulled away, her head spinning. A smile curled on her lips when she turned around. She let her fingers play over his chest, feeling the chiseled lines of his abdomen. They headed lower and dipped into the waistband of his leather pants.

Lugh drew in a sharp breath and waited for her. One snap. Then another came undone. All she had left was the zipper, and she would have her reward. The zipper came down slowly. His pants hung loose around his hips and revealed his engorged cock. Before she could claim her prize, he grabbed her hand. She frowned.

"Are you going to make me beg?"

"Of course not. But I want to have some fun."

Kalliope wasn't exactly sure what that meant, but by the amused gleam in his eyes, she figured it was going to be excruciatingly wonderful. He snapped his fingers and she found she was back on the bed. Only this time, when she tried to move, her hands were tied above her. Her legs were attached to the bedposts, and she was naked. "Sometimes I hate it when you take advantage of me."

He stood beside her, also naked, with something over his hand. "I can always untie you, but I don't think it's me taking advantage of you. You can always tell me no." He kissed her nose. He snapped his fingers again and then blackness covered her eyes. Something soft ran over her breasts, some kind of fur, but when he pressed down, she felt sharp spikes grating over her flesh. The mixture of the fur and the spikes made her jump and then cry out. The pain was minimal, but when he stopped, she wanted more.

Next, something cold was placed on her nipples. There was pressure and then the metal got tighter and tighter. Lugh had never played this way with her before, and she liked it. He stopped letting her nipples adjust to the ache. The pleasure of the pain made her wet. Something tickled the bottoms of her feet. She began to squirm in the restraints.

"Stop. Please." She writhed and tried to get away from whatever device tormented her.

"As you wish," he breathed next to her ear.

His hands ran over her exposed flesh, stopping to touch the top of her breast, then her stomach, and then tangled in the curls of her down. His hands slid under her legs and gripped the mounds of her ass. He spread her legs further apart. When the first stroke of his tongue hit her clit, her back arched off the bed. She clenched the restraints until her palms were numb. The flicks on her throbbing bud were slow. He savored each stroke. Each time he touched her, her body was electrified with pleasure. He tightened his grip on her ass and kept her grounded. Kalliope didn't know how long she could keep this up. He would bring her to the precipice of the orgasm, but wouldn't let her jump off. He left her hovering. His tongue plunged deep into her well, but that wasn't enough.

The need to have him buried inside of her was consuming her reason. Her eyes were squeezed so tight that they hurt. She gritted her teeth and tried to bring her body back into sync with her mind, but it wasn't obeying. Her heart raced. Sweat had broken out on her flesh from his slow laves. This was torture of the ultimate kind. She sensed he was using his power to build her to new heights, but keep her from coming.

He touched her again and began to suckle her clit and nibble at it. That did it. She couldn't take it anymore. The sensations were too intense between the wetness of his tongue and the suction of his mouth against the sensitive flesh of her folds.

"I need you inside me. Can't…ahh." She held onto the rope and was surprised it didn't break. Her toes gripped the end of the bed. The combinations of his manipulations and the aching from her nipples made it challenging to concentrate. All she knew was that if she didn't get him soon, she was going to lose her mind.

In that instance, she was able to see again. Lugh was above her with his hands under her shoulders. She could move her legs and wrapped them around his waist. "You taste so good." He kissed her so she could taste her tang. She deepened the kiss until their tongues met once again. At that moment, Lugh slid inside of her, hitting her buried clit.

Kalliope quivered from the intensity of the friction between them. She bit his lips and then kissed the side of his neck. The yearning to hold him ran through her mind. When it did, the bindings disappeared, and she was able to wrap her arms around him. She buried her head in his shoulder, marveling that they were together once more. Her heart had been healed. He pumped into her fast, increasing the rhythm between them. She ran the soles of her feet over his firm butt, feeling the muscles in them bunching. He was getting ready to come.

"I love you," he whispered.

"I love you, too," she responded.

When she did, the world exploded in colors. Stars streaked across the expanse of her mind. She was sucked into Lugh's power and saw the vast universe before her. Her body was racked with quivers of ecstasy as she came and he stayed buried inside of her. He kissed her cheek and then her lips, making her semi-aware of her body. The more he stroked her, and mumbled to her, the faster she came back to herself. Lugh rolled over and settled next to her on the bed.

She trailed her fingers over his strong jaw, still marveling over the fact that he was alive and with her. Her thoughts brought her back to the first time they had been in bed. He had been in her dream, and he was giving her a massage. Of course, when she woke up, he was still there, naked, in all his glory.

"What is it?" He kissed the inside of her palm.

"Nothing. Everything. You. Me. All of this. Everything that's happened since we first met. Since I called the cops on you. When you were chained up in Hephaestus's hall. The girls are real witches now. Theresa has the twins. I have a familiar somewhere, and now I have you. I'm so thankful for that. What are the others going to say when they know you're back?"

"Who cares what they say? Nothing else matters to me in this world other than you. I'm tired of all the games that the gods play. The first time around, you were involved out of circumstance, the second because you made a promise to Dagda, and this last time because you said you would help Anubis. No longer. That was another condition I gave All Hail. The gods' rules don't apply to you anymore. I don't want you put in harm's way ever again." He drew her up in his arms and hugged her tight. She knew he was telling the truth, and that was a comfort. She was tired of being bound by Universal Law.

"I appreciate that." Her hands roved over the muscles in his back and to the perfect mounds of his butt cheeks. She pinched him so that he jumped, and then she slapped him.

"What was that for?"

"I promised the others I would go to Avalon tonight since they were celebrating. The night's almost gone, and I would like to go. However, I need you to zap me over there since I'm out of magick."

He rolled his eyes and then got up. "I guess I can give you up for one night." He snapped his fingers and she was dressed again in her witch costume. Only this time, she had a red corset over the black dress that barely covered her breasts.

"I hope you made it so I'm not popping out of this."

He ran his fingers over the tops of her breasts. "Oh, you'll pop out of it later. I'm not done with you tonight."

A zap of power rolled through her. She moaned from the small orgasm that crested inside of her. If she hadn't promised the others she would go, then she would have stayed here with him and let Lugh have his way with her. "And what are you going as?"

He gave her a wicked grin and then snapped his fingers. Instead of him being naked, he was now covered in white and yellowed fraying linen bandages. The only things that were visible on him were his eyes and his mouth, with a little slit for his nose.

She groaned. "A mummy! Seriously?"

He held out his arms and walked toward her slowly. "Come… kiss…your…mummy."

She punched him in the shoulder as hard as she could. "You're so paying for this. You have to swear to me after tonight, no more mummy jokes. I've had enough of them."

"As…you…wish."

A whoosh of air surrounded them and they were gone.

Chapter Eighteen

When they appeared, the party was in full swing on Avalon. A large bonfire burned at the center of the Tor. Jack O' Lanterns lined the paths all along Avalon leading into the forests and to the houses. A large table with goodies and food was laid out on the bottom of the path. Dagda's self-playing harp strummed "Monster Mash." Anubis was at a microphone growling along, and the three fates were singing backup. The power of the place overwhelmed her. She had never been here without magick. Part of her missed it now.

No. I can't think that way. My magick was sacrificed to bring Lugh back to me. Any forfeit was an ample price to pay. He squeezed her arm. She smiled at him. Priestesses and other gods were mingling here and there. The fey queen snuggled up to Dustbunny. When she saw Kalliope, she gave her a thumb's up. She returned the gesture. Theresa and her coven were talking with their dates. Her coven sisters were each dressed in priestess garb, a white shift, and pentacles at their throats. Humphrey hovered between them near the twins. When he saw her, his eyes grew wide and he zoomed over. His jaw dropped and his eyes fixated on her busting cleavage. She saw a line of drool begin to trail down his lips.

"Ahh, Humph. My eyes are not in my chest."

He gazed up at her and said something, but all she heard was the croaking of a bullfrog. He waited for a response, but she glanced at Lugh.

"Don't worry, love."

She felt a touch of his power warm her and then all the odd squeaks and growls that were voices became understandable to her.

"Thanks."

"No worries."

"What did you say, Humph? I couldn't hear you with Anubis howling over there."

The drool string was longer. She put her finger under his chin and moved it up. "Please let me love them. Luscious and so plump. One touch and I swear I'll be good."

"It's good to see you, too. Go back and watch the twins." She kissed him on the nose and then headed toward Theresa. "So what did I miss?"

The three women, who had been joined by Nas and her date, all stopped talking.

"Where have you been?"

"We expected you hours ago."

"I had something to take care of."

"Yeah, more like someone," Nas muttered. "Lugh's not even cold, and you're off screwing someone else."

Kalliope bit her tongue to keep from laughing. She elbowed Lugh and realized he must have been concealing his power so the others wouldn't know. She glanced at the dates of her coven sisters and saw they were other Celtic gods, but she wasn't sure exactly who they were. All three of them were almost indistinguishable except one had red hair, the one with his arm around Adele had black hair, and the one closest to Anna was silver-haired.

"Nas, I didn't know that I wasn't allowed to be with someone else since Lugh was gone. I mean, I've dealt with his passing. He would want me to be happy."

"I thought you were more broken up about the whole thing. He loved you with his whole being and you aren't even—"

She felt the heat of the Lugh's power blasting against her. He was getting angry. "Nas, for the love of all the gods, let it rest. Can't Kalliope be happy?"

All of the other gods stopped. Nas's mouth dropped. The bandages on Lugh's head exploded in flame, leaving his face free. The goddess rushed into his arms and he hugged her. Kalliope felt a stab of jealously, but knew that Lugh was over Nas. He patted her back and then pulled away.

"How did you do it? How…you were dead! No god can come back from that!"

Lugh wound his arm around Kalliope's waist. "Kalli gave up all her magick and a little slice of her soul to bring me back. Thanks to Azrael and Anubis, I am alive again."

"You're mortal?" Flidais asked behind her.

She turned. "I am."

"I thought after eating the apples, the magick was ingrained in you and couldn't be taken away?" the goddess asked.

"It couldn't unless there was an extreme case and she was willing." Dagda appeared next to the goddess dressed in a business suit. "Do you like my costume?"

"Let me guess, you're a stock broker."

He laughed. "No. I'm a layer."

Kalliope glanced at Flidais. "He means lawyer."

"So that means after everything you went through and gave us magick, now you don't have any? It's not fair," Theresa exclaimed.

"It's fine, honestly. I'll have you guys coming in and raiding my cabinets. Lugh will always be with me, and I doubt the others are going to give up on me because I'm mortal. Besides, Excalibur is still attached to me. That connection didn't slip, so that gives me a little bit of magick by default, I guess. The most important thing is that Lugh's alive." She hugged him, and he kissed her lightly on the lips. Her soul sighed.

"Go with the others and have some fun. You deserve it."

She nodded and wandered back toward the houses. When she did, she came upon Morgaine sitting with the fey queen next to her brother's grave. Fresh flowers had been placed on the stones. The sorceress looked up when she saw her.

"Dressing up a as witch on Samhain? Isn't that a little bit past your time, being a goddess and all?"

Morgaine didn't know.

The fey queen smiled. "The lords of the dead heard you."

"Yeah, they did. Thank you."

"You're welcome. Oh, you left this on the island." The fairy queen handed her the wreath of flowers she had given her from before.

"Thanks." The lavender flowers were still perfect and none of the petals had come off.

"What was she talking about?" Morgaine asked.

"Lugh is back from the dead, and it took all my magick to do it."

"Wow. No wonder you feel different. Are you happy?"

"I'm ecstatic. I can't tell you how it feels to have him here. I'd do it all over again. I wanted to thank you for being my friend these past couple of years. I hope that you don't ditch me now that I'm not witchy."

"I'm not going to break up with you because of something like that. Why don't you come back with me and enjoy the festivities? We have hours to party. Or is your mind wandering to other things? You know the one thing that's going to suck is that you won't be conjuring those penis-shaped oranges anymore."

Kalliope giggled. "I think I can live with that."

They made their way back to the party. She took in all the sights around her and was amazed at all the different costumes. One of the gods was dressed up as a banana. Another one was dressed like a cheesecake, and she thought it was David at first, but the strawberry topping on the face of the cheesecake was dripping on the ground. David would never be that sloppy. She did spy the cheesecake god flirting with a group of priestesses. He had a silver platter and was feeding them samples of chocolate cheesecake.

"David, you're not feeding them your special brownie cheesecake, are you?" Kalliope teased.

He turned toward her, and she heard one of the other priestesses sigh because he was turning away from them. She understood because he had an overwhelming effect on women. His smile widened, and he offered her the cheesecake. "This is only chocolate cheesecake. No brownies. I swear. Taste." He placed the tidbit on her tongue.

Once the chocolate hit her, it melted on her tongue. She curled her toes and savored the delicacy he offered her. It was almost better than sex with Lugh, so she knew it was amazing. "Thanks."

He took her hand and kissed it. "Thank you for saving the others and my ass. I didn't enjoy having my energy sucked out of me. I really hate vampire spiders, especially those who don't enjoy cheesecake."

She giggled and shook her head. Scanning the rest of the partiers, she saw Lugh searching the crowd. He seemed distraught. She wrapped her arm around his waist and snuggled against him. She felt his uncertainty and wasn't sure what was wrong. *"What's the matter, love?"*

He sighed and ran his fingers through his hair. *"I see you around the other gods, and I don't like David flirting with you. Or you being away from me. Not after what happened."*

Kalliope sensed his jealousy. This was a first. She gazed into his eyes. "I only love you. I'll always love you no matter how wonderful his cheesecake is. You should know that." She rested her hand on his chest. She leaned up and kissed him, focusing all her love into the gesture. She was rewarded with a shiver from him. It was nice to know that even though she didn't have any magick, she was able to make him shake.

"I know. And…" He got down on one knee and took her hand. "Will you marry me here?"

She was taken aback. "Now?"

"Yes, now. Unless you really want the big wedding with the cooing doves and Zeus shooting lightning bolts over our heads."

"No. I don't really care about any of that. Honestly, I think his aim is a little off. I only wanted to be sure that I didn't offend anyone if I didn't invite them. It's not like I get married to a god every day. But I don't have a dress and—"

"We could get married naked. I know I don't mind, but—" He waggled his eyebrows at her.

"Ahh. No. Please, not dressed like that at least."

He glanced down at his mummy costume and gave her a pout with an evil gleam in his eye. He moved his hand over his body, and his clothes changed. He was now before her in a suede sleeveless vest, a god toque around his neck, and soft black pants with a sword buckled at his side. His bare arms showed the blue dragon tattoos wound around them. A thin gold circlet sat upon is head. Lugh held up his hand. "Excuse me everyone."

The music stopped. Silence encompassed the whole of Avalon. Even the wind stilled. "Would it be agreeable to all those in attendance if Kalliope and I married among such wonderful friends and family?"

Kalliope glanced at the faces of her friends and the other goddesses. Her Aunt Constance was in the back, surrounded by a soft glow. A large smile spread on her face. No one said anything until Dagda stepped forward. "Is this what you both want? Because, you know, I was hoping you'd have coffee at the wedding, and you've disappointed me. I don't think I can stay." He had a solemn expression, but then after a moment, he broke into laughter. "It's about time you guys got hitched." He snapped his fingers and was dressed exactly like Lugh, except the dragons on his arms were moving. Chairs appeared out of nowhere for the guests. The muses began to hum an ethereal melody along with the self-playing harp.

Kalliope felt power surround her. When she looked down, she was no longer in the witch's costume, but a white dress falling around her in layers. Silver chimes were sewn into the skirt so when she moved, she jingled. Her hair was different, and when she felt her head, the wreath of flowers the fey queen had given her was wound in her hair. There was a thin veil over her face. The dress bodice laced up the front and was tied with blue ribbon. Around her throat was the coolness of the pentacle she'd had. Morgaine slipped off one of her rings and slid it onto Kalliope's finger.

"Now you have one of each. Something old, something new, something borrowed, and something blue." She hugged her and then conjured a mirror.

"Thanks." Kalliope was amazed. What she saw staring back at her was a fairy princess. Tears lined her eyes. She was getting married. She really wanted her parents to be there to see her. That had always been one of her dreams. She nodded, and the mirror disappeared. Lugh squeezed her arm.

"Ready?"

"Yeah."

He snapped his fingers, and in his hand were two rings. One was thicker than the other, but each was braided silver and gold. He handed her the larger one. "Gold for the god, and silver for the goddess, because that's what you'll always be to me."

The harp began strumming the wedding march and Anubis began singing. It turned out he had a great baritone. Lugh walked a few feet ahead of her to stand before Dagda.

Kalliope felt on the spot and naked without anyone to walk her down the aisle. Someone slipped their arm through hers. When she checked, she saw her father.

"Hi, sweetie. Your mother and I wouldn't miss this for all the world."

She gave him a quick hug. Her mother sat in the row right behind them and waved. Kalliope waved back before turning to face Lugh. "Okay."

Her father began to lead her down the aisle. When they got to Lugh, he stopped. "You'd better take care of her."

Kalliope nearly laughed at the statement. The god grew serious. "You have my word, sir."

"Okay then. You look beautiful." Her father took his seat by her mother.

Her heart sped up, her mind not believing she was getting married. It was overwhelming, but it was wonderful. She glanced up at the sky. Stars began streaking across the darkness. There were hundreds of them.

"What is that?"

"I think it's all the hearts I've broken."

"Not even you have *that* many admirers."

He gave her a playful smile. "You want to bet?"

She was going to say something when Dagda blatantly coughed to get their attention. She turned to him. Lugh held her hands in his.

"Dear friends, we are gathered here to witness the union of my beloved grandson Lugh and his beloved bride

Kalliope, who we have all come to know and love. We stand upon the great Isle of Avalon with all of our close friends and family. These two have overcome great adversities to be together. Is there anyone among you that wishes to speak against this union?"

Kalliope held her breath and peered into Lugh's deep green eyes. In his gaze, she saw trepidation. She squeezed his hands and sent her reassurance. Before her jaunt in Egypt, they had the approval of all the other major pantheons except the Egyptian one, and now that Isis was out of the picture, she figured they were okay. The moment extended a little bit longer until she heard Dagda take in a breath to say something.

"Ahem!"

She glanced behind her to see a small man with a bald head and black, round glasses standing in the aisle. He was dressed in a T-shirt that was too long for him that sported Strawberry Shortcake being speared by a unicorn. He had on khaki shorts and no shoes. There was even a paper under his arm. She giggled at the T-shirt. Everyone around her grew very quiet and still. Lugh's eyes widened and he went to one knee. Everyone bowed before this small man. He tugged on her hand, but she ignored him.

"No need to bow. I didn't come here for that. I wanted to see the new bride for myself." He walked toward her slowly. Even as he advanced, she felt his awesome power hitting her.

"Who are you?"

He gave her a little smile. "You call me All Hail, which I find quite amusing, actually."

Her body went cold. "Oh God. I mean…ahh. Crap. I never meant—"

He chuckled. "I know. It's quite amusing. My real name is Mortimer, but you can call me Morty. I don't intend on stopping the ceremony, but I wanted to see you in person to see who has been riling up all the gods these past three years. You've broken some amazing Universal Laws, you know. There was a while there I thought you might take your new powers and try to come after me. Lugh, you've made an excellent choice for a wife."

"Thanks, Morty."

"Hey, Mort. Long time no see. Are you ever going to lift that ban on caffeine?" Dagda asked.

"I will if you stop popping into Times Square and turning yourself into a palm tree."

Dagda's face fell. "But I like waving at people."

Mortimer shook his head and took her hand. His hands were warm, and he seemed to glow from the inside out. "Don't worry about anything. My promise to Lugh stands. You won't be bound by Universal Law anymore. That is my wedding present to you for saving my ass last year. Just make sure you keep an eye on him. I don't want him in Summerland again." He patted her hand and then walked by them. When he did, she felt a pinch on her butt that made her jump. Kalliope watched him fade out.

"Well, that was interesting. It's not every day he makes an appearance here," Dagda commented. "Shall we get on with it?"

"Please do," Lugh responded.

He took their hands again and wrapped a piece of braided leather around them. "With this cord, I unite your souls in love and perfect trust. Nothing shall sever this link between you. Do you Lugh Draco Solaris take Kalliope Isabella Danvers to be your wife?"

"I do."

"Do you Kalliope Isabella Danvers take Lugh Draco Solaris to be your husband?"

Kalliope held her breath and felt the anxiety coming from Lugh. "I do." At that moment, she felt something tug on her soul. When she looked at the leather on their hands, it was gone.

Lugh picked up her left hand. "I give you this ring as symbol of my undying love. You are the air I breathe, and I am happy to call you my wife." He slid the ring onto her finger.

She noticed that unlike his, hers had small diamonds embedded into the braiding. All of them were red. Parts of his heart. The ring fit her perfectly. She took his hand and slid his ring on his left hand.

"I give you this ring as a symbol of my everlasting love. You are the man of my dreams, naked and all, and I am happy to call you my husband."

"Well, kiss the bride."

Lugh smirked, but picked up her veil. He tilted her chin up and pressed his lips against hers. His hands slid along her hips and then over her butt. He squeezed her derriere. Kalliope returned the kiss with fervor, feeling how excited he was. He fed images of them alone in their hideaway, running around naked and having marathon lovemaking sessions. She laughed, and he put her down. When they faced the audience, everyone erupted in clapping and cheers. There wasn't a dry eye in the place.

Humphrey flapped over to her. "That was beautiful." He sniffled.

"Humph, you're too much. Go eat some cheesecake. I see your froggy girlfriend over there." Kalliope waved at the other frog that hovered by David. She batted her long lashes at Humphrey when he got closer.

Lugh ran his hand down her back. "It seems like your familiar has a friend. And your coven is seeing the brothers. They're good guys. Dagda and Flidais are happy. You're finally mine."

Kalliope pressed herself against him. "Don't think because we're married that means I start doing housework and am counted as one of your possessions."

"I would never think that. You're so much more than that."

"Really, what am I then?"

He kissed her lightly. "I'm not going to tell you now. I thought I'd wait until we were both naked and I had a chance to use those penis-shaped oranges you so love."

"What if I want the real thing?"

"You can have that too. Anytime you want."

"Promise?" She ran her hand over the bulge in his pants.

"Promise."

"Good, 'cause I'm feeling a little frisky."

"Well then, let's ditch the wedding and I can show you exactly how much I enjoy you being my wife."

"All in good time." She squeezed his rigid shaft and gave him a devilish smile.

"You're such a witch."

"I know. And that's why you married me."

Epilogue

Kalliope stood over her candle making pot, dipping a wick into the hot wax. She had been making candles for a couple of hours, and it was slow going. The store was insane. Orders hardly stayed on the shelves, no matter how much inventory she had. Whenever she thought she was ahead, she was really behind because Theresa and the girls were calling in orders at least once a day, and the Internet site was getting hits all day.

From her vantage point, she could see Humphrey and his froggy girlfriend, Julip, lounging on the couch, flipping through the television stations. They made her pause whenever she saw them using their webbed feet to navigate the stations. Lugh's greyhound snoozed on the couch, keeping a protective eye on the twins since she was babysitting. Not that she expected anything supernatural to get through the circle she had in the living room. Her powers might have been gone, but the crystals she supercharged hadn't lost any of their power. When they sensed danger, the barrier went up automatically.

When the candles were to the thickness she desired, she hung them over a dowel so they could dry with the other pairs of candles that she had made. She stared at the boxes on the table and sighed. This was one of those times she missed her magick. It would've been so much easier to zap the boxes full and get them over to the store. Now she had to drag them down to the car and then drive over.

Not that she minded, and Lugh would do it for her if she asked, but she didn't want to bug him about the trivial things. It was one thing when they went to their place in the other realm, but it was another when she asked him to take her to the store because she forgot to get something. She didn't want him to think she was taking advantage of him.

Her mind wandered to her husband's wonderfully shaped derriere and his ever at attention equipment. On their honeymoon, she hadn't gotten out of bed for three days. He kept torturing her with pleasure until she was a pile of ooze. When she couldn't take anymore, he let her recover and began all over again. He made her pancakes and fed her chocolate. He massaged her whenever she wanted and never complained about their life together. Some part of her wondered if he would ever tire of her, but then she looked at her wedding band with the red stones and knew he wouldn't.

Suddenly, she sniffed and smelled smoke. The burnt smell broke her out of her reverie. Fire had erupted on her stove. She'd left a towel too close to the burner. She reached to pull it away from the flame and burned her hand.

"Ouch. Crap!" Quickly, she turned the faucet on and plunged her hand into the cold water. It offered some relief.

"You called, madam." Lugh smiled, but when he saw her holding her palm to her body, his expression grew grim. "Let me see."

"It's nothing." The burn throbbed.

"It's not nothing, Kalli." He gently took her hand and unfurled her fingers. Her skin was red and starting to pucker, forming a blister. He ran his hand over the wounds. She jumped from the sudden pain, but then the ache vanished. Lugh kissed her fingers and the center of her palm before taking her into his arms.

"Thanks."

"What am I going to do if you hurt yourself worse? What happens if you get into a car accident and I don't get there fast enough? I don't know if I can keep you away from

Azrael again. I was able to keep him away from you when you died last year."

She buried her head in his shoulder. The idea of dying and leaving him again wasn't something she wanted to fathom, but they'd had this conversation before. Eventually, she would die. Without her magick, she was completely human. "It will happen. I'll come back, and you'll find me again."

"But you won't be *my* Kalliope. Your spirit will be the same, but no. I won't have it." He let her go, trailing his fingers down her face. Before she could speak, he was gone.

"Is everything okay?" Julip asked in her southern drawl.

"Yeah. Thanks. Did you guys need anything?"

The frog flapped closer to her. "Your man sure is a fine piece of man. Too bad he's already taken."

Kalliope laughed at hearing the frog lust after her husband. "What would you do with him anyway?"

Jullip's eyes grew large. She licked her lips. "Oh once you go green, you don't go back."

Kalliope shook her head and focused on her candles. She had two more wicks left, which were four candles. She lifted another and began to dip when she heard something rustling behind her. There was someone with her, but it wasn't dangerous because her wards didn't go up.

"Your appleberry candles smell wonderful. I thought you might want something to eat." Constance had an apple pie in her hands.

She licked her lips. The thought of apple pie whetted her appetite. She hadn't had one in awhile, and her aunt made the best pies. She turned down the burners and took the pie. She got out a plate and cut a slice. The caramel color of the half gooey apples made her even hungrier. She'd been working most of the afternoon and hadn't stopped for lunch. Once she dug into the pie, the apples oozed out of the sides. Her stomach growled again. She ate the pie and noticed the apples were sourer than normal, but she didn't think much of it and ate the piece.

When she was done, she licked her lips and eyed the pie. "Thanks. It's good. So, what brings you here?"

"I wanted to see how you were holding up. I haven't seen you since the wedding and I figured maybe there was a little one on the way."

She snorted. "I don't think so. But I'm happy."

Constance scooped up another piece of pie for her. She dug into it, and by the time she finished the second piece, she was feeling a little dizzy. Putting her hand to her head, she attributed it to eating too fast.

"Are you okay, dear?"

"I think so, but I'm going to lie down for awhile. Can you watch the twins?" She stabbed her fork into another piece of pie. After swallowing, it made her even dizzier. She headed into the bedroom, scarcely able to keep her footing. The world began swimming. Before making it to the bed, she tripped over her feet and then landed on something soft. She opened her eyes enough to see she was in her bed at their house. Before she could do anymore, sleep dragged her under.

"Sweetie!"

She stirred and opened her eyes. The world around her was more focused than what she remembered. The air was crisper. Lugh sat on the bed next to her. It felt like she had woken from a long illness, but her head was still fuzzy. "Hey. How did I get here?"

He smiled. "I didn't bring you here. You came yourself."

Her brow furrowed. "How is that possible?"

"How many pieces of pie did you have?"

"A couple, why?"

"I think you overloaded on apples."

Kalliope was about to say something when it dawned on her. "Those weren't regular apples in the pie, were they?"

"Nope. Dagda gave Constance the apples to make the pie with."

She sat up slowly. "Are you sure? I thought I wasn't allowed to eat them anymore. I mean, I don't want to get anyone in trouble."

He took her in his arms. "You're not. Calm yourself. Everyone misses you. They like you being feisty, but as Dagda puts it, he misses your spunk."

"How many apples were in that pie? Last time, I ate three of them and I was a normal witch. Flidais ate five and she went back to being a goddess."

Lugh smoothed the hair from her head. "There are seven apples in the pie all together. You won't become a goddess, but you won't be a witch either. You'll be the way you were before when I healed you and brought you back from the dead. Only because I don't expect you to eat the whole pie."

"Why, you don't want me to get fat?"

"No. I adore Constance's pies. I was hoping you'd save me a piece." He snapped his fingers and a plate with two pieces of pie appeared on the bed. "Eat the third slice and then let your body rest. I'd say one more after that will cinch it."

He cut a piece of apple in half and speared it with his fork before bringing it to her lips. She ate it, suddenly feeling hungry again. "How long was I asleep?"

"A day or so. Magickal overload will do that." He began to eat his pie.

Kalliope stared at the pie, glad that the others liked her so much they wanted her back to her old self. After a moment, she dug in and devoured it. She waited a second and had a feeling of dizziness, but it wasn't as bad as before. A flush of warmth went through her. The world came into sharper focus. The air was sweeter. She could sense Lugh's mood more and see the glow in his skin.

Taking a deep breath, she wanted to put the magick to the test. In her mind, she thought of Morgaine and envisioned her in the middle of getting hot and heavy with one of her boy toys. An evil thought ran through her mind. She saw penis-shaped oranges raining down on the sorceress. After a moment, she heard a scream echoing through the astral realm. To make sure, she glanced at Lugh and saw he was dressed. She snapped her fingers and immediately, he was naked.

"Oh, I like this side of you. I missed it." He ran his hand over her sides and her breasts.

"Are you going to start getting frisky with me?"

He kissed her neck, making her moan. "I'd love you to, but you might want to eat the other piece of pie before it gets cold."

She rolled her eyes, but took the plate. Even though the pie was good, she was full and wasn't about to romp around in the bed. She finished the piece and got up. Heading to the window, she stared out at the expanse and saw the beauty around her. Already the power of the apples was tingling inside of her. Knowing that, she also knew she wasn't human anymore. At least not in the sense that she was going to die. She would have forever with Lugh now.

He wrapped his arms around her waist and rested his head on her shoulder. "How are you feeling?"

"Good. I was thinking about something and wanted to know how you felt about it."

He kissed her neck. "What was that?"

Her hands slid over his. "How do you feel about a family?"

His surprise rolled through her. "You're not…are you?"

She chuckled. "No. Not yet, but I've been thinking about it. You said that we both had to be willing." She turned in his arms and saw he had gone white. "I didn't know if that was something you wanted to think about."

Lugh took a step backward and did the unthinkable. He fainted dead away. Kalliope broke out into a giggling fit seeing him passed out on the floor. She knelt down and tried to revive him. Seeing the look on his face was priceless. Contemplating the idea of children was an interesting one, but it was another adventure that she could deal with. Now that she had her magick back, the possibilities were endless.

A smile turned on her lips as she thought about the future. All she could think was—

Oh my!

About the Author

Crymsyn Hart is a bestselling author of erotic romance. Her worlds are filled with luscious vampires, gorgeous gods, quirky witches, and everything else that goes bump in the night. Crymsyn worked as a psychic for many years in Boston while attending Emerson College. She graduated with a BFA in Writing, Literature, & Publishing. Crymsyn shares her life with a small zoo, two playful puppies, and her hubby Mark. If you come after dark, you're more than likely to find her snuggled up with a gory horror movie or a bloody vampire movie. Crymsyn has a collection of Living Dead Dolls and five bookshelves overflowing with books. Of course, there's always room for more.

Visit her on the web at:
www.RavynHart.com

PURPLE SWORD PUBLICATIONS
Romantic Speculative Fiction
www.purplesword.com